The Montana Cowboy's Heart

The Montana Cowboy's Heart

A Cole Brothers Romance

Kaylie Newell

The Montana Cowboy's Heart

Tule Publishing First Printing, August 2021

The Tule Publishing, Inc.

First Publication by Tule Publishing 2021

Cover design by Erin Dameron-Hill

ISBN: 978-1-954894-45-7

Dedication

I wouldn't have been able to finish this book without my critique partner, Nola. She is gone but will be with me always. Love you, friend.

K.

Chapter One

PORTER COLE LEANED against the paddock fence and looked out over the group of sixth graders with his Stetson pulled low over his eyes. He was only half listening to his twin brother go on and on about dude ranch technicalities—how many guests they were expecting this fall, how they weather-proofed the barn, *blah, blah, blah*. Brooks had a tendency to ramble, especially when he was talking to kids. It was like he had this boredom radar. Whenever he sensed that anyone younger than fifteen could be halfway interested, he had to age at least thirty years and start talking about the most mind-numbing things. *Exhibit A...caulking.*

Porter rubbed the back of his neck. No, what kids this age wanted to hear about was the gross stuff. The stuff they could elbow each other in the ribs about, while laughing behind their hands. If Porter was giving this speech, he'd probably start out with cattle worming, and go from there.

"And that's how we keep things nice and dry for the animals," Brooks finished, looking pleased with himself. "Any questions?"

Spindly arms shot up like weeds in a garden.

"Yes," Brooks said. "You in the blue."

"Does it always smell so bad out here?"

"Well, it kind of does. But you get used to it."

The kids murmured in agreement.

"Yes. You?"

"Are you a real cowboy?"

"I am."

There was a collective *ooohhh* that moved through the squirmy group.

"You, right over there."

"Do you rodeo?"

This from a boy who was standing off by himself. His small, freckled face looked sad and hopeful at the same time. Porter watched him, watched how his pretty, young teacher reached out and put a hand on his shoulder, as if she knew why he'd asked this particular question.

"No," Brooks said, "I don't, but I have friends who do. Anyone else?"

Brooks continued answering questions—did they have any baby animals on the ranch? Did horses sleep standing up? Is it true that you can burn cow patties, because my uncle said you could…

Their small voices faded into the background, as Porter kept an eye on the little boy and his teacher. She leaned down to say something in his ear, but he didn't answer. His shoulders looked stiff, his back rigid—like he was carrying a weight.

She straightened, brushing her dark, wavy hair away from her face, and moved over to another student who was doing the potty dance. Her teacher's assistant had already taken a small group to the bathroom, but still hadn't reappeared.

Porter was about to offer himself but looked over when the redheaded boy shoved another boy in the arm.

"Take that back!"

"Knock it off, runt."

And that was it. Before Porter could stop him, the smaller boy launched himself at the bigger boy, and they fell into a tangle of boys in the dirt. And probably some manure, too.

The kids squealed. "Fight! Fight!"

Porter lunged forward, grabbing the redheaded kid by his jacket and yanking him off. But not before the bigger boy got a solid smack in. Blood trickled from the smaller boy's nose, and he wiped it furiously away with the back of his hand.

The teacher helped the other kid up, and they all stood there stunned.

"He pushed me!" the bigger boy cried.

"Because you called me an *orphan*. I'm not an *orphan*, you jackass!"

"Cat!" This from their teacher who shot him a warning look. "That's enough."

"Tell *him* that's enough."

"Why don't you go back to Missoula already?" The bigger boy stood there breathing hard. He was especially stunned. Probably because he hadn't expected to be tackled by a kid half his size.

Porter and the teacher locked gazes. She looked apologetic. Maybe embarrassed that her field trip had gone south so fast. She didn't need to be. Porter was used to all kinds of mishaps on these adventures. Last month a first grader had fallen and chipped her tooth on her own boot. He still had no idea how that was even possible.

Behind him, Brooks had managed to corral the kids and interest them in something other than the lingering drama of the fight. The history of Diamond in the Rough Dude Ranch, and how its original settler had been a real-life gunfighter. Porter guessed that'd be enough to keep them occupied for the next five minutes or so.

The teacher stared down at the boy she'd called Cat and frowned. "I think that might be broken."

Porter didn't think so. He'd seen a lot of broken noses in his time, his own included. But it wouldn't hurt to get it checked out, just in case.

"Should we call his parents?" he asked.

"He doesn't *have* any parents," the bigger boy mumbled, brushing off his jeans.

"Alec," the teacher bit out. "Go." She pointed toward the group of other students. "We'll talk about this later. I'm going to have to call your mom."

Alec glowered at the ground and shuffled off.

Looking back at Porter, she took a steadying breath. "I'm actually Cat's guardian at the moment," she said. "He's my student, but he's also staying with me."

Huh. Interesting. Porter glanced down at the boy, who was staring at his scuffed tennis shoes. His shoulders were hunched, his red hair sticking up in the back. There was a tag poking out of his jacket, askew, like it was recovering from the excitement of the morning, too.

Porter touched his elbow. "We should probably take you to the doctor, just to make sure that thing isn't broken."

The boy shrugged. "Sure."

"I can drive you," Porter said, glancing back at the teacher. "We'll be back here before they have their lunch."

"I'll need to tell Becky. She's still in the bathroom with the kids."

"I don't care if it's crooked," Cat said. "My dad has a crooked nose."

"Yes, but probably not because he wanted one." His teacher looked up at Porter again. "I'm Justine, by the way. Justine Banks."

Porter shook her hand. Her skin was powdery soft, and surprisingly warm in the crisp morning air. But her grip was firm, no-nonsense. "Porter Cole," he said. "Nice to meet you."

"And this is Cat."

"Cool name."

The boy was still staring at his shoes, so Justine clarified for him. "Because he's scrappy," she said quietly. "His real name is Tom. You know…tomcat…"

Porter smiled at that. "It fits," he said. And it did. This kid was a pistol. But he also seemed melancholy. Whoever his dad was, *wherever* his dad was, it was obviously a tender subject in his young heart. Porter understood this, as his own complicated father had been a tender subject his entire childhood.

"I'll go pull the truck around," he said.

Justine Banks, the pretty teacher with eyes the color of the Montana sky above, smiled. And he saw then that she wasn't just pretty, she was actually stunning. "Okay," she said. "Thank you."

His heart skipped a beat. As far as middle school field trips went, this was turning out to be a humdinger.

JUSTINE CLUTCHED THE throw blanket to her stomach and looked down at Cat, who was watching TV with his chin in his hands. He was small for his age, his red hair permanently messed-up. He looked like he'd just come inside from a windstorm, but he'd actually just gotten out of the shower. Apparently, it dried that way. His freckles were scattered across his cheeks like confetti—as if someone had tossed them there, and they'd stuck. He was an adorable child, but Justine was used to adorable children. Being a teacher had desensitized her to things like freckled cheeks and cowlicks. It was the inside of a person that really counted. And inside, Tom Roberson was damaged.

That undisputable fact did something to her that she hadn't been prepared for when her dearest friend had asked for a favor this summer. What was supposed to have been a few weeks, had turned into a few months. And if Justine was being honest with herself, if they were *all* being honest with themselves, it was looking like Cat wasn't going home to Missoula anytime soon.

She held out the blanket, resisting the urge to wrap him up in it like a burrito. His thin arms looked cold sticking out of his worn T-shirt, and he wasn't wearing any socks. Her 1920's bungalow had a tendency to get chilly in the evenings, and tonight was no exception, with an early fall storm brewing outside.

"Hey, Apollo Creed. Want this?"

He smiled, not showing any teeth, as usual. Those smiles were rare, but she'd gotten a few. She coveted them. There was a faint, dark smudge below one of his blue eyes. His nose hadn't been broken after all, and he'd avoided the worst of a shiner, but it still looked sore.

He was a tough little guy though, and gazing down at him now, her heart swelled. She didn't want it to swell. In fact, she hadn't meant to get attached at all. Justine had a busy job. Maybe not so busy a social life, but still. She'd been offered a dream job teaching in the UK next year, thanks to her connections with a college girlfriend, and she was planning on saying goodbye to Marietta, her sister, and her dad, in the summer. At least temporarily. And now it was looking like she was going to be saying goodbye to Cat, too, which filled her with a sense of sadness that unsettled her.

"Thanks," he said, and reached for the blanket.

Justine picked up the remote and turned down the cartoon, *Phineas and Ferb,* his favorite—then sat next to him with a sigh. He smelled like baby shampoo. When he'd first come to stay with her, there hadn't been much notice. She'd gone shopping in a rush and had grabbed random things off the shelf, not thinking it would matter much. Now, all these weeks later, he was still using the economy bottle that boasted *no more tears*, and if he minded, he never said so out loud.

"Hey," she said. "Are you ready to talk about today?"

Frowning, he looked at the TV. "There's nothing to talk about."

"Cat. I think there is."

"He started it."

"But you didn't have to finish it. You know better."

Actually, she wasn't sure he did. Just because she was now his guardian, didn't mean he'd absorbed any of her lectures. He was a lost boy, looking preoccupied at the moment, and older than his years. He had good reason. His mom had died when he was in kindergarten, and he hadn't seen his father since he was a toddler. Nola, Justine's teaching mentor from Missoula, was his maternal grandmother, and had official custody. She'd done a wonderful job of raising him so far, but now, even that home had been turned upside down. Poor Cat. Except for Nola, and now Justine, he really didn't have a soul in the world.

So, did he believe there were better ways to settle an argument than with his fists? No. Probably not.

Justine sighed. "I'm just glad that Alec's parents were so understanding. They could've pushed for suspension."

At the mention of Alec's parents, Cat winced. It was small, almost imperceptible, but she caught it.

"Alec James is a big, fat turd."

His tone was so matter-of-fact, that Justine had to bite her lip to keep from laughing. It was true. Alec was a bully. He was big and rotten, and mean as a snake. But Cat still shouldn't have tackled him.

"Cat…"

"I know. I shouldn't fight."

She knew he was struggling with this and wished for the hundredth time that there was some way to reach him. To touch what was hurting inside. But he was far away, locked inside his own little bunker where people and circumstances couldn't hurt him. She identified with this more than he knew.

"Did you call Porter?" he asked suddenly.

She blinked at that. She hadn't known he'd been paying much attention to her conversation with the tall, green-eyed cowboy who'd driven them to urgent care that morning. She'd been trying to hide her own reaction to Porter Cole for the better part of that hour, since it involved sweaty palms and a fluttery heartbeat that was very *un*-Justine.

"I don't…I didn't…"

Cat eyed her, clearly not going to let her off the hook that easy. Porter had asked her to let him know how Cat's nose was. Justine decided that was just a nice thing he'd said, and she hadn't planned on following through. He made her nervous, and Justine didn't like being nervous. She liked being calm and cool and in control. It was what had protected her from most of life's messiness up to this point. If you were cool as a cucumber, as her dad liked to put it, people kept their distance. Easy peasy.

"You said you would," Cat said.

"I know. But I don't think I kept his number." It was a stretch, and she knew it.

"Google the ranch's number."

"I guess I could…"

"You know who his dad is, right?"

She knew. She hadn't known that Cat did, though.

"Eddie Cole," Cat went on, answering his own question. "Isn't that weird? Don't you think he kind of looks like him?"

Justine did think he looked like his famous rock star father, who'd retired in Marietta to open a music store. Mistletoe Music. Just another reason Porter made her nervous. Tall, dark, and sexy, *with* celebrity roots.

"Will you call him, Justine?" Cat asked. For whatever reason, this was important to him. And he'd been let down enough lately.

"Okay."

"Right now?"

She laughed. "*Okay*, okay. What's the rush?"

"I just don't want him to think you forgot."

"You're right. I'm sure he wants to know how you are."

She sat there stalling for a minute, but Cat watched her closely. Taking a deep breath, she got up and pulled her sweater close, feeling butterflies bump around in her lower belly. This was ridiculous. Porter Cole was just a guy. A really handsome and charming guy, but just a guy.

"Your phone's over on the kitchen table," Cat said.

"Thank you."

"Now is probably a good time because it's right after dinner."

"Right. Thanks."

"You can go into the bedroom for some privacy. I don't mind."

She paused, watching him. It was an adult-like thing for an eleven-year-old to say, but she also knew he'd probably overheard too many conversations regarding his well-being lately. Or lack thereof.

"I'll just be in the other room, then," she said. "Alright?"

"Alright."

"There's some mint chocolate chip in the freezer when you're ready."

"Okay."

"Does your nose hurt? Do you need a Tylenol?"

He smiled at her. This time with teeth. And a dimple. "I'm *fine*."

"Alright." She tapped the phone against her thigh. "I'll be right back."

She reminded herself that as far as cucumbers went, she had a reputation for being the coolest of them all.

Easy peasy.

Chapter Two

"SHE'S GONNA SCRATCH the hell out of him," Brooks said. "And when she does, I don't want to hear a word about it."

Porter gave his brother a cocky smile from across the ranch house's rustic living room. A fire crackled from the river rock hearth, and a gusty wind rattled the big, dark windows.

At his feet, his border collie, Clifford, was in the middle of an epic stare-down with Brooks's fat black farm cat, Elvira. They hated each other. Always a good time.

"I don't know," Daisy said, her stocking feet tucked underneath her robe-clad bottom. His brother's girlfriend looked like a greeting card with her steaming cup of hot chocolate hovering at her lips. "I'm betting on Clifford tonight. He's feeling his oats."

"If that's what he's feeling," Brooks replied flatly, "we need to rethink what we feed him. He stinks."

Porter laughed. They really should call it a night. They had a group coming in from Bozeman in the morning, and the cattle had to be fed before that, which meant dawn patrol.

But honestly, the living room with the dark leather couches and colorful, southwestern-print area rugs felt cozy and warm. His own small guesthouse next to the barn was cold and empty in comparison.

He put his feet on the edge of the heavy wood coffee table and looked over at the fire. It had been a long day. A strange day, with the middle school field trip that had turned into something resembling a Las Vegas prize fight. *Justine Banks…* The teacher's name kept nagging at him. He actually knew a Banks. His physical therapist's fiancée was one Jemma Banks, whose sister had moved here from Missoula last year.

He rubbed the stubble on his chin. Thanks to Marietta being such a small town, information like this was as free-flowing as its river with the same name. He'd talked to Jemma at the Mistletoe and Montana Christmas tree auction last year, and she'd mentioned being excited that her sister was settling in, and her family would be together for the holidays.

So, if this was the same sister, Justine was relatively new to town. He knew that much. And she was beautiful, he knew that, too. He also knew she'd taken in a little boy who liked to fight and wanted a crooked nose just like his dad.

He sighed. "Well…I'm gonna hit the hay."

"It's eight thirty, grandpa," Brooks said.

"I know what time it is, and I also know how it's going

to feel when my alarm wakes my ass up at five."

"Don't pay any attention to him, Porter," Daisy said, taking a sip of her cocoa. "He's usually asleep by nine. And snoring."

"I don't snore."

"Okay, babe."

Porter stood with a grunt. "Good night, asshole. Good night, Daisy. Clifford, come on."

The dog looked up, but not before getting a bat on the nose from Elvira. A parting gift that elicited a surprised yelp.

"Ha!" Brooks slapped his thigh. "Told ya."

"You need to get a life, brother."

Porter walked over to the coatrack where his Stetson hung, and his knees popped. Shit, he did sound geriatric. Sometimes he wondered how long he'd be able to keep this up. This breakneck pace of trying to run a working ranch and a business at the same time. Other men his age were starting to slow down, starting to settle down, with wives and kids. Families to keep them grounded. Porter had grown up watching his father run from relationship to relationship, trying to find that soft place to land, only to fall flat on his face. *Nope.* Porter had decided a long time ago that he wasn't going to chase anyone or anything. Nothing was worth that kind of heartache.

Clifford trotted after him, his nails clicking on the hardwood floor. From the kitchen, the old wall phone rang, its hollow *bringgg!* reverberating through the house.

"I'll get it," Brooks said.

Porter grabbed his hat and jammed it on his head—then put his Carhartt jacket on and turned the collar up. Outside, the wind whipped the trees back and forth, and the wind chimes were going batshit crazy. If this kept up, they might get some early snow.

Turning, he tipped his hat at Daisy. "See you tomorrow."

"Good night. Sleep tight."

He opened the door to a frigid blast of air and a few stinging drops of rain.

"Porter," Brooks said behind him. "Wait. It's for you."

Frowning, he looked over at his brother who had the receiver stretched from the kitchen. Nobody he knew would be calling the main house at this time of night.

"I probably got myself on some kind of list," he mumbled. "Tell them I'm out?"

Brooks put the phone back to his ear. "He's not in right now." Then after a pause, "Alright, I'll let him know. And it's Banks?"

"Whoa, whoa, whoa," Porter said, reaching out his hand.

"Uh, one second…" Brooks held the receiver to his chest. "I thought you said you were out."

"I was."

Brooks grinned. That dumb grin he'd had since the ninth grade. "Ahh. Grandpa's in love."

Porter shoved him and snatched the phone away. "Shut

up."

He hoped to God she hadn't heard that. Normally, when it came to his fraternal twin, he was the juvenile delinquent in the relationship. But tonight, Brooks was giving him a run for his money.

He cleared his throat. "Hello?"

"Porter?"

"Yeah. Hi."

"I'm sorry to call so late, but I was getting Cat settled, and then I realized I'd lost your cell number, and, well…" Her voice was soft on the other end of the line. A little sexy. But she also sounded measured, like she was checking this phone call off her to-do list and was ready to move on to the next thing.

He switched the phone to his other ear and turned his back on Brooks and Daisy, who were now staring at him from the couch.

"Don't be sorry," he said. "I'm glad you called. How's our prize fighter?"

She laughed. "He's alright. The beginnings of a black eye, but I don't think it'll be too bad."

"We should see the other guy, right?"

"Yeah. Unfortunately, with these kinds of things, Cat usually comes away the most banged up."

"He's pretty small," Porter said.

"Too small to be picking fights with kids twice his size. But he always jumps first, thinks later. I'm trying to get him to stop that, but it's a process."

"And how's his nose?"

"Well, it's not broken at least..." There was a pause on the other end of the line. He could hear a television in the background, but it was faint. Justine took an audible breath before finishing her sentence. "It's his heart that I'm most worried about."

Porter had known this kid had baggage. It was written all over his freckled face. None of his business of course, but there was a strange pull to know more. Maybe because he identified with Cat on some level. He'd longed for his father as a kid, too. And he and his brothers had also been taken in by someone else. It was a crappy club to belong to, but belong, they did.

Leaning against the wall, he looked out the dark window over the sink. Something was banging against the house, probably a shutter to one of the upstairs windows. Clifford laid down on the linoleum and put his head on his paws with a sigh. Loyal as the day was long.

"So, this happens often?" Porter asked, hoping she'd keep talking, wanting to know, but also enjoying the sound of her voice too much to hang up yet.

"Yes, it does," she said quietly. "He's had a rough go of it."

"I'm sorry. I remember how hard middle school was."

"Yeah. Me, too."

There were a few seconds of silence, and Porter looked

down at Clifford, thinking he should probably just let her go before it got awkward. But before he could, she spoke again.

"I know who your dad is," Justine said. "I can't imagine being a preteen on top of having a parent as famous as yours."

He smiled. "Yeah. It was interesting. My mom took off, and he tried raising us himself, but the rock and roll lifestyle and fatherhood didn't really gel. That's when he sent us to Marietta to live with our aunt. Got in a lot of fights that first year when I was trying to figure it out. Only I didn't have the right hook that Cat has."

"He's fearless. It's a blessing and a curse. I'm worried that one of these days he's going to get really hurt." She paused. "His mom died. And his dad…well, we're not sure where he is. On the rodeo circuit somewhere. Or at least that's what I've heard through the grapevine. Cat keeps old pictures in his room."

Porter remembered him asking Brooks about the rodeo. It made sense now. Brooks had told him he knew guys on the circuit, and that was true. They both did. He frowned, mentally listing all the cowboys he could think of with red hair and a guilty conscience.

"Anyway," Justine continued, "I'm hoping to get him settled in with me. His grandmother is a teaching friend of mine from Missoula. She's going through cancer treatments right now and needed some help."

"You're a good friend."

"Well…I really love her. And Cat's a great kid."

"He's going to be with you for a while then?"

She paused again, and he could hear her soft, even breaths on the other end of the line. "Probably until the end of the school year. I've accepted a position to teach overseas in the fall."

Porter's stomach knotted at the words. He didn't really know why. He didn't even know this woman. But he'd be lying if he said he didn't want to *get* to know her. And that wouldn't exactly be convenient from across the Atlantic.

Just as well, he thought. He wasn't in the market for getting to know someone better anyway. That always led to talk of relationships and settling down, and all those things he'd made a career of avoiding. Best to end this phone call with a *thanks for calling, hope Cat feels better soon*, and hang up. He had a long day tomorrow.

Instead, he cleared his throat.

"You know," he said, "when I was his age, a family friend brought me out to her ranch, introduced me to the horses, to the animals, and it was the best thing that ever happened to me."

"Mmm…" He could almost see her nodding thoughtfully at this. "I've heard working with horses can be really good for some kids."

"It's because they don't expect anything from you, don't bring anything to the table except love. That's it."

Justine was quiet on the other end of the line. Thinking

maybe. Maybe picturing Cat trying to take charge of a thousand-pound animal, or buck hay onto the back of a truck. Porter had seen smaller guys do it. It was amazing what the body was capable of if the heart wanted it badly enough.

"What do you say to Cat coming out here to work after school?" he asked evenly. "In exchange for some horseback riding lessons?"

"Oh…I…"

"Just think about it. His schoolwork would come first, of course, and I have no idea if he's doing sports, which wouldn't leave much time for the ranch. But I can tell you that I've seen kids blossom out here. Come into their own. Especially if they're struggling with other things."

"We could just pay for the lessons…"

"You could. But working for them is better. It would give him a sense of accomplishment and pride. At least, that's how I ended up feeling. And I can tell you, it was worth it."

"You *do* own a ranch now."

"Exactly."

"Cowboys are his heroes. We can thank his dad for that."

"Well, not all cowboys are heroic, but I get it."

She sighed, and he wondered if those delicate brows of hers were furrowed. He imagined running his thumb along one of them before he could help it.

"Are you sure you've got time for this?" she asked. "With

everything else you have going on out there?"

"That's what my brother is for," Porter said with a shrug. He could practically feel the weight of Brooks's stare from behind him. "And the ranch hands. We're headed into the slow season, so actually, it'd be the perfect time."

Justine was quiet for a few seconds. "Okay," she finally said. "I think this would be great for him. Thank you so much."

Porter felt a slow smile spread across his mouth. And this time, it didn't have anything to do with the fact that he was going to be seeing Justine Banks again. This time, it had everything to do with the scrappy little kid who was missing his dad, and who had no idea that his childhood was about to take a turn for the better.

Porter would bet his Stetson on it.

Chapter Three

JUSTINE DROVE DOWN the long gravel drive as slowly as possible, trying her best to avoid the potholes. Her small hatchback wasn't used to anything that wasn't paved. Actually, to be more accurate, *she* wasn't used to anything that wasn't paved. She could smell the sweet scent of grass and hay through the cracked sunroof, and it made her stomach dip. She'd grown up in Montana, but when it came to the country, she always felt like a fish out of water. She was more of a city girl. At least, that's what she'd always told herself.

She looked over at Cat, who had his nose pressed to the window. He hadn't said much on the way out, but she could tell he was excited about this. What she'd told Porter the other night was true—he idolized his father, at least, what he knew of him, and the prospect of spending time on a working ranch made him feel closer to him somehow.

"We'll have to make sure your homework doesn't suffer," she'd said.

He'd nodded eagerly at that, unphased.

"And Porter brought up a good point—if you want to

play any sports, it might be hard to find the time with lessons in the mix."

"I don't want to play sports," he'd said evenly. "I want to ride bulls."

Justine had watched him, trying not to let her feelings show. He was so desperate to be just like his dad, and it wasn't her place to take that away from him. But there was no denying the rush of protectiveness she felt at the hopeful, innocent look on his face.

He turned to her now, his strawberry-blond eyebrows raised. "Do you think I'll get to ride today?"

She smiled, looking back at the road. "I'm assuming you mean a horse and not a bull?"

"I wonder if they have any bulls out here."

"Probably. But probably not for riding."

"You don't think Porter has ever tried?"

In Cat's mind, all grown men had either attempted riding a bull, or wanted to. Naturally.

"I don't know," she said. "It's a good question, though."

She pictured the long-legged cowboy with the warm eyes. He had a muscular, athletic build. He looked like he could ride a bull. Actually, he looked like he could do pretty much anything he set his mind to. Justine felt her heart thump tellingly against her rib cage. She couldn't help it. She was human, and he was gorgeous.

In the distance, the log cabin-style ranch house came into view. It had been a landmark in Marietta for close to a century, changing owners a handful of times before the Cole brothers had bought it a few years ago. They had painstakingly restored it to its former glory, or at least that's what the brochures in town said. Justine had always been fascinated with Diamond in the Rough because of the history behind it. She was a sucker for history.

Seeming to read her mind, Cat leaned forward to peer at the house. "It looks old."

"It is old."

"Like something in a western movie."

She could see it, too. Cowboys from a century ago, clomping up the porch steps with their spurs jangling. Smoke curling from the chimney, the smell of cooking meat, bacon, and backstrap, wafting through the chilly Montana air.

"This house was built a long time ago," she said in her best teacher's voice. "Do you know when?"

Cat wrinkled his nose. "Nineteen-fifty…*seven.*"

"Older than that, even. Nineteen-twenty."

"That's ancient."

"Well, not ancient exactly, but definitely old."

"Before cars?"

"There were cars," she said, "but a lot of people still rode horses. It was an in-between time when the world was going through a lot of changes. And it was right after the first World War, so people were finding their new normal…"

Cat nodded politely but turned his face back to the window. She'd lost him with her history lesson. She should've strategically placed Jesse James in there for good measure.

"The barn is pretty," he said.

She looked over as she pulled into the driveway. It *was* pretty, like a postcard with Copper Mountain rising so majestically in the distance. The Marietta River wound close by, giving the property a lovely Ansel Adams feel. She could only imagine how stunning it would look over Christmas, blanketed in snow.

She put the car in park and turned off the engine just as Porter appeared, walking down the porch steps with a friendly wave. He looked extra rugged this afternoon in a red flannel shirt and an old denim jacket. He wore Wranglers, of course, and boots that looked like they'd seen better days. And his Stetson. A black hat pulled low over his eyes, shielding them from the bright, midday sun.

She turned to Cat, but he was already out the door, ruffling the ears of a little black and white dog who'd appeared out of nowhere.

Justine unbuckled her seat belt and climbed out after him. The air smelled tangy, like animals, and she pulled it into her lungs. She could see why people booked vacations out here. She wasn't necessarily a country girl, but she could see how relaxing it might be, how therapeutic.

Which, of course, was exactly why they were here.

She turned to Porter who was standing with his thumbs hooked in his belt loops. "That's Clifford," he said to Cat.

"He loves kids."

Cat knelt in the dirt, letting the dog lick his face. "Does he work cows?"

"He does. And he eats cow patties, so be careful with that tongue."

Cat made a face but wrapped his arms around the dog anyway.

In the afternoon sunshine, he looked more pale than usual. Smaller. But no doubt, happier, too.

Porter touched the brim of his hat. "Miss Banks."

She smiled at the playful formality, trying to keep her heart in check. "Mr. Cole."

"Do you have any bulls out here?" Cat asked, standing up, but keeping a hand on Clifford's head.

"We have one, and his name is Alloy. He's huge and he smells."

"Can we see him?"

"We can do better than that," Porter said. "He loves apples. Want to feed him one?"

"Sure!"

"He's in that paddock off to the side of the barn over there. We need to keep him away from the ladies at the moment. He's not pleased."

"Can I go over now?"

"Lead the way. But wait for me before you go up to the fence, okay? I'll grab the apples."

Cat took off with the dog at his heels.

Tucking her hands into the pockets of her wool peacoat, Justine watched them go. "I haven't seen him like that…" She paused, thinking about it. "Well, maybe ever."

Porter walked up beside her, and she told herself she was probably just imagining the heat coming off his body. But she most definitely was *not* imagining the smell of the soap he'd used that morning, maybe even his shampoo. And her belly tightened.

"I think it might be love at first sight," he said.

"Oh…sorry?"

"Cat," he said. "And this place."

Her cheeks warmed. "Oh. Yes. For sure."

"What did you think I meant?"

"Nothing!"

He smiled down at her. She wasn't used to being teased. She knew she put out a certain vibe where men were concerned. Serious, a little brooding. After her dad had left her mother, she'd gotten very good at analyzing people's motives, whether or not they were going to stick around, whether or not she should allow herself to care. That wariness had only grown over the years and had made it next to impossible to trust anyone with any degree of certainty.

She tucked her chin into her scarf. Even so, it felt good to be teased a little. Like warming her hands next to an open flame.

Porter began walking, and she fell in step beside him. Their shoes crunched over the gravel drive, and a horse whinnied from one of the pastures to their left, taking her focus off her pounding heart.

"So, I have to be honest," Porter said, staring straight ahead at Cat, who was throwing a stick for Clifford. "I'm happy to see you again, Miss Banks."

This was why her heart was pounding. This right here. She snuck a look at him, at his strong, handsome profile, and had to assume he talked to all women like this. He was a charmer. And she was falling for it, hook, line, and sinker.

She straightened her shoulders, determined to get her feet back on solid ground. "And why's that?"

"Isn't it obvious?"

"Not to me."

"Well, all I can say is that none of my teachers looked like you when I was a kid."

At that, she stopped and turned to him with a smile. It was almost impossible not to smile around this guy. Which would only encourage the flirting. She could see it might be a never-ending cycle.

"Are you trying to get on my good side?" she asked evenly.

"Is it working?"

"I don't know yet." *Lie.* It was definitely working.

He put his hands in his pockets and rocked back on his boots, glancing over to make sure Cat and Clifford were waiting for them. They'd stopped to pick up another stick. Clifford barked twice before Cat threw it a country mile. He had a good arm.

When Porter looked back, his expression was more serious. He licked his lips. "Hey, I just wanted to run something by you while Cat's out of earshot."

"What's that?"

"You said his dad was on the circuit."

Her heartbeat slowed. Nobody had heard from Cat's father, a young, wild redhead, for a few years now.

"He was," she said. "The last Nola knew."

"Well, I was thinking about it the other night. Brooks and I know several guys who rodeo. It's a small world, and you make a lot of acquaintances in this business. I put two and two together… Is his name Calvin? Calvin Roberson?"

Justine watched him. "Yes…"

"I heard he's traveling with a group of cowboys that are headed back here for the stock auction before Thanksgiving. It's a big draw, and the friend I talked to said Roberson's in the market for a new horse. He'll be in Marietta in a few months."

It wasn't often that Justine was at a loss for words. She usually had something to say about nearly everything. But here, now, she was speechless. Cat's father. The one who was so nomadic, he couldn't be bothered to stay put and raise his own son, or make sure that Cat's grandmother was holding up okay. Which she absolutely wasn't.

She took a steadying breath. "Oh."

"Is he not allowed to see Cat?"

"It's not that he's not allowed…" She let her voice trail off. When it came right down to it, she wasn't sure what was allowed and what wasn't. Nola hadn't gone into Cat's abandonment in depth, concentrating on the here and now, and the very real issue of getting him settled somewhere for the school year. For the second time that day, Justine was reminded of the fact that as soon as he got settled, he'd be looking at another upheaval again, when she moved to the UK.

"Listen," Porter said, watching her closely, "I definitely won't mention it to Cat. I just thought it was more an issue of you not being able to find him, that's all."

"It was. Kind of. But the truth is, it's more than that. Cat's desperate to see his dad again, but his dad doesn't exactly seem desperate to see him."

"You're worried he'll get hurt. It makes perfect sense."

"Yes."

"Don't sweat it then. He doesn't have to know."

She frowned, considering this. "Even if we don't tell him, he could find out from someone else. Marietta is a small town. Word is bound to get back to him eventually."

She glanced over at Cat. He was now giving Clifford a belly rub, the dog's tail sweeping back and forth in the dirt like a feather duster. The magical lure of the bull seemed temporarily forgotten.

"Then again," she continued quietly, "if his dad comes through town, and he finds out that I knew and didn't tell him, he'd never forgive me."

"What do you think his grandma would say? Your friend?"

"I'm not sure. She's got her hands full with treatments, and I know this would make her anxious. But I guess I'll need to tell her. It's not really my decision to make." She paused when the breeze pushed a strand of hair over her eyes. Tucking it behind her ear again, she looked up at Porter. "But I'll be honest, I don't have any use for that guy. What kind of horse's ass walks out on their son?"

A shadow passed over Porter's face, and she wished she could suck the words back in. She remembered him telling her that his mom had run off. And of course, his dad had sent him to Montana to be raised by his aunt.

"I'm sorry," she said softly. "I didn't mean that."

"Of course you did. It's true."

"I know things like this aren't always black and white," she said. "Sometimes people have issues they can't get past; sometimes they think their kids are better off without them. And there's a lot of truth in that kind of thinking. I just...well." She shrugged. "I have my own abandonment issues that tend to color my viewpoint. So, there's that."

They started walking toward the barn, but slower this time. Like neither one of them wanted to stop talking.

"Your dad?" Porter asked.

She nodded. "He left my mom when my little sister and I were in high school. It was awful. Sometimes I look at Cat and see how much he loves his dad, when I couldn't even stand thinking about my own. It took a while to get over it. I didn't speak to him for years. It was only recently that we made up, and my sister and I moved here to be close to him."

"That's a happily ever after."

She smiled. "It's a happy for now, I guess. Remember, I'm leaving next year."

He kicked at the gravel with his boot. "And I was just starting to like you."

"You don't even know me. I can be a handful."

Turning to her, he winked. "Do tell."

Before she could fumble a reply, Cat waved from the paddock.

"He's ready for his apple!"

Sure enough, a giant red bull was standing at the fence, looking interested in whatever might be coming his way in the form of boys bearing fruit.

Porter waved back. "Be right there!"

"I really can't thank you enough for this," Justine said. "He's so excited."

"Well, talk to me after he's mucked out his first stall. He might not be as excited then."

"Don't worry. He's not afraid of work. Or getting dirty."

Justine watched the boy bend to pet the dog at his feet, his red hair sticking up in the back. She breathed in the musky scent of the man walking beside her and felt the warmth of the autumn sun on the back of her neck. And felt more content than she had in a long, long time.

Chapter Four

"SO WAIT A minute..." Porter's dad said. He shifted from his spot on the dark leather sofa and set his beer on the table next to him. His leather pants kept sticking to the couch and making this god-awful squeaking sound. "What kind of fair is this again?"

Porter didn't turn around. Just kept adjusting the collar of his white western shirt in the mirror. Griffin answered for him.

"It's a science fair," his brother said, nursing his own beer. "And Dad, can't you put a blanket down or something? That *sound.* It's like a cat giving birth."

Eddie Cole ignored that. Instead, he leaned back and touched the chains nestled in his chest hair, as if making sure they were still there. "Can I come?"

At that, Porter did turn around. "*What?* No way. Absolutely not."

"Why?"

Griffin laughed.

"Fine. I'll change the pants. I'll go incognito."

"Dad," Porter said, running a hand through his hair.

He'd actually put product in it tonight. He couldn't remember what the hell he'd been thinking. "You've never managed incognito in your life."

"That's not true. I went to the Stroll last year. Nobody noticed for half an hour."

"And then you gathered a crowd outside Rae's food truck," Griffin said. "They nearly knocked it over trying to get pictures, remember?"

Porter smiled. He remembered. It had been Marietta's first introduction to the over-the-hill rock star who would end up retiring within its city limits. Not long after, *the* Eddie Cole, the one with the famous Christmas hit from the nineties, had opened a music store on Main Street and things had died down a little. Not much, but a little. Even so, Porter had no doubt that if his dad showed up at Marietta Middle School tonight to see Cat's science project, pandemonium would ensue.

His father crossed his leather-clad legs and rubbed Clifford's belly. The dog was lying beside him, and automatically lifted his front paw for better access.

"Are you *pouting*?" Griffin asked.

"No. I just want to go, that's all. I've heard a lot about this kid over the last few weeks. I think I'd like him."

"That's exactly why you need to stay as far away as possible," Porter said, picking up his Stetson. The stupid gel Griffin had talked him into would only make his hat ring worse. If that was even possible. "You know if you came, it wouldn't be about Cat anymore. It'd be about you."

"Then again," Griffin said, adjusting his dark-framed glasses, "what would we have done if David Lee Roth had shown up at one of our school functions?" Griffin was the polar opposite of his older twin brothers. An accountant, who could probably land a modeling gig, if he really wanted to.

"Not helping," Porter mumbled.

Jamming his hat onto his head, he turned back to his reflection with a critical eye. He looked exactly the same as he did every day. The only difference was, his shirt was clean. Perfect.

"Why'd you put the hat on?" Griffin asked. "You just messed up your hair."

"I never should've listened to you. I haven't used gel since high school. Now it actually *looks* like I'm in high school."

"Smells good, though." This from their dad, who was now running his hand through his own shaggy blond hair.

Porter turned around. "You can *smell* me? From over there?"

"Don't flip out," Griffin said calmly. "You're just used to smelling like horse. Tonight, you actually smell like you showered."

Porter shot him a look.

"Seriously, though," Griffin said, "Justine will appreciate it."

A slow heat crept up Porter's neck, and he resisted the urge to loosen his collar.

"I think you're into her," Griffin continued. "And you're not used to being into anyone, so that's why you went overboard on the gel tonight. I told you a pea-sized amount. Only *pea*-sized."

Porter choked down a laugh. Funny because it was true. Not that there was any chance in hell he'd admit it to his little brother and his dad, who were both staring at him like he was standing there clutching a dozen roses, instead of the keys to his truck.

"Thank you for that insight, Doctor Phil," he said evenly.

Griffin shrugged.

"So, are you two yahoos just going to stay in my house and drink beer in it all night without me?"

They looked at each other.

"Right," Porter said. "Just let Clifford out before you leave, and don't forget to lock the door."

His father raised his beer in the air. "Have fun!"

JUSTINE ADJUSTED HER Marietta Bobcats sweatshirt over her jeans and scanned the school library. It was a full house tonight—families and friends milling around the science projects that had been so carefully set up around the large room. It smelled like coffee and pumpkin bread. Little brothers and sisters peeked through the legs of their parents, while older siblings stood proudly by their work, explaining the process to anyone passing by.

It was a great turnout for a school function, which made Justine happy. But there was still one person who hadn't shown up that she'd been hoping to see.

Swallowing hard, she looked over at Cat, who was showing the school custodian his da Vinci bridge that he'd built out of pencils. The idea had been to learn about gravity, force, and friction. And of course, to see how much weight it would hold. Cat looked serious and a little out of place in his brand-new polo and khakis that Justine had bought him for tonight. His red hair was combed neatly to the side, and he kept looking at the door, like he was expecting someone in particular. Which he was.

Justine glanced at her watch, trying not to obsess about it, but obsessing anyway. Since Cat had come to stay with her, she'd been slowly building an unrealistic bubble around him. Anticipating future pain and disappointments, and trying to avoid them as much as possible. Deep down, she knew that was a losing battle, of course. It was impossible not to be disappointed by life, by the people who drifted in and out of it. But the desire to shield him was still there, and as she grew more attached, the stronger it became.

"Wow," said a soft voice behind her. "This is pretty amazing, sis."

Smiling, she turned to see her sister Jemma standing there. She wore a Christmas sweater with tiny jingle bells sewn to the antlers. Of course she did. Jemma loved Christmas.

But it hadn't always been that way. When Justine's dad walked out, it had been right before Christmas, and she and Jemma had struggled with the holidays ever since. But living in Marietta was healing for them. Not only had they finally forgiven their father, but they'd also been reintroduced to the Christmas magic of their childhoods. It was hard not to go overboard in a town that made you feel like you were living inside a snow globe.

But then again, it was September.

Justine flicked one of the bells on Jemma's sweater, and it tinkled merrily.

"I know," Jemma said. "I know. But I can't help it."

"Nobody's asking you to."

"But I can feel your judgment."

"No judgment here."

"Uh huh."

Justine grinned and pulled her baby sister into a hug. "You're so sweet to come. Did you have to get off work early?"

"Just a few minutes. Where is he?" Jemma asked, looking around. "I know he's got the best project here."

"You're not allowed to say that."

"But it's true. You know it's true."

"I'm his teacher. I know he's brilliant. But so are all my students."

Jemma poked her in the ribs. "Come on," she whispered. "Just admit he's the smartest."

"*Stop!*" she whispered back.

"Miss Banks…"

They both glanced down at a little girl with unruly blond curls. She looked concerned. "My grandpa wants to know if the coffee is decaf. He said if it's not decaf, he'll be up all night."

"You can tell him its decaf, Eugenia. It's alright."

The girl hurried off to relay this message to an elderly gentleman across the room.

"I don't know how you do it," Jemma said, shaking her head. "All these small people looking to you for answers."

"Well, regular or decaf isn't exactly rocket science."

"You know what I mean."

"It helps that I love them so much. It's such a sweet age."

Two little boys began shoving each other a few feet away. "He farted!" one of them cried. They both dissolved into laughter before a weary-looking woman, presumably their mother, yanked on their shirt collars to separate them.

"So sweet," Jemma said.

"Middle school boys are just…easily entertained."

"That's a nice way to put it."

Justine glanced at her watch again.

"He's still not here, huh?"

She didn't look at her sister. She was afraid if she did, Jemma would be able to read her like a book.

"No. I'm just worried about Cat." *True. Mostly.*

They glanced over to where he stood across the room, all by himself now, as people filed past.

Justine sighed. "Poor little guy."

"He's tougher than he looks."

"I know. But there's so much to unpack there. I wish I could make it better for him."

"Well, I'm no expert," Jemma said, "but I think you are. Having him here in Marietta with you is huge."

"Until I leave next fall. And what about Nola? What if she doesn't get better?"

Frowning, Jemma touched her elbow. "You can't do that to yourself. Take it as it comes, right? And in the meantime, he's out at Diamond in the Rough. That's a good thing. And…hey. Don't turn around, but your cowboy Prince Charming just walked through the door."

Justine's heartbeat skipped at that.

"Wow," Jemma said. "I forgot how hot he is."

Jemma already knew Porter. In fact, she knew his brothers, too. Since she'd lived in Marietta longer, she had a jump on the social scene here. Not that Justine had ever been that social, but still.

"He's coming this way," Jemma said. "And in those jeans, too."

Justine ran her hands down her thighs and wasn't surprised to find that her palms were damp. Porter made her feel like she was seventeen again.

"Justine?" she heard him say.

Steeling herself, she looked over. And he nearly took her breath away. Justine wasn't normally swayed by handsome men. In her experience, good looks usually came with a healthy dose of conceit. But Porter's looks also came with the kindest eyes she thought she'd ever seen.

"Hey, there!" she said. "You made it."

"Sorry I'm late. There was an accident on the highway, and I stopped to see if they needed any help."

"I hope nobody was hurt."

"Nope. They'll just have a headache in the morning. Hey, Jemma." Porter reached out to take Jemma's hand. His arm brushed Justine's in the process, and she imagined sparks crackling between them, bright and popping like on the Fourth of July.

"Hey, Porter." Jemma smiled her biggest smile. She obviously couldn't help it. This was what happened in his presence. "Good to see you again."

"You two look alike," he said. "I almost couldn't tell you apart from across the room."

"This, coming from a twin," Jemma said.

He shrugged. "Fraternal. And everyone knows I'm the better looking one anyway." He winked at them, and Justine felt tingly all over.

"So," he said, "where's the man of the hour?"

"He's over there. By the pencil bridge."

Porter's dark brows shot up. "He made that? By himself?"

"He did. He's super proud of it."

"I couldn't even build Legos as a kid."

"He'll be so happy you're here," Justine said. "He's been excited to show you."

"Well, better not keep him waiting, then." He took his Stetson off and ran a hand through his dark hair. "Ladies."

Before they could recover enough to reply, he was walking through the crowd, almost a foot taller than most of the other men in the room.

"*That*," said Jemma, "is a work of art."

Justine stared after him. He was beautiful, no doubt about that. But at the moment, all she cared about was how good he was to Cat.

Her heart squeezed. It was impossible not to see how much Cat adored him. Which was a blessing and a curse. Porter hadn't let him down yet; it was too soon for that, really. But what if he did? Could Cat really take another disappointment right now?

Jemma stepped up beside her. "Uh oh. What's that look for?"

"What look?"

"That look. The one you're giving those two."

"I'm not giving them any look." That wasn't true. She knew she was.

"It's okay for him to get attached, you know," Jemma said softly.

"I just remember how I felt after Dad left. I think I'm always going to struggle with that. At least on some level."

"You don't trust men," Jemma said matter-of-factly. "Childhood trauma is legit. I get it."

"But look at you. You went through the same crap I did, and you and EJ are in this great relationship. You've forgiven Dad..."

"So have you."

"Yes, but forgiving doesn't mean forgetting. Look at Cat. He's going to have the same issues with people, and it breaks my heart."

"Well, maybe not," Jemma said. "Maybe he'll have a completely different experience. Look at tonight. Porter promised he'd come, and he showed up. Even if he was a little late."

Justine nodded, considering this.

"And, sis..." Jemma put an arm around her. "I didn't trust EJ overnight. I had to work at it. And I had to work at forgiving Dad, too. It's a process."

Justine looked over at Porter, who was now kneeling next to the da Vinci bridge and listening intently to whatever Cat was saying. *It's a process.* Learning to trust people absolutely was. She thought of Cat's bull rider father, who at that very minute was breaking his son's heart, and reminded herself that she should call Nola and tell her that Calvin was going to be in town. Her friend was wise in the ways of the world. She'd know exactly what to tell Cat. Or what *not* to tell Cat about his dad.

"You're right," she said to her sister. "But it's easier said than done."

Chapter Five

PORTER LEANED AGAINST the barn door, watching Cat muck out the stall a few feet away. Abby, Brooks's pregnant little mare, stood behind the boy like a dog, gently nudging his shoulder every now and then for a pat. Cat would always oblige, turning to scratch her ears or underneath her fuzzy chin like he'd been doing this all his life.

Porter smiled. He'd known the work would be good for him, but it was turning out to be even better than he'd thought. Learning how to ride horses was only a small part of loving them. Taking care of them formed a bond that was the backbone of the give-and-take relationship between man and animal. Abby had been the perfect introduction to this lesson. She loved people, especially kids, and seemed to have a built-in sensor for the ones who needed her most. She was going to be a wonderful mother.

She nudged Cat again, this time nibbling on the back of his windbreaker. She'd found the tag a few minutes ago and was now making a game of it.

He laughed and ducked away. "Stop!"

"I think she likes you," Porter said. "Or your jacket tastes like hay. Either, or."

Cat leaned on the rake for a second to catch his breath. His mop of red hair had fallen over one eye, and he pushed it away absentmindedly. "When is she going to have her baby?"

"Soon. I'd say in the next few weeks or so."

"I wish I could be here when she has it." He reached over and ran his hand down her neck, his fingers disappearing underneath her thick black mane.

"I bet we could arrange that."

Cat's eyes widened. "Really?"

"Sure. As long as you're not in school at the time. We'll talk to Justine to see if I can come into town and pick you up when Abby's time comes, okay?"

"Even if it's in the middle of the night?"

"Even then."

"Wow. Thanks, Porter."

Cat looked away then and frowned. Something crossed his face, before he dipped his head and picked up the rake again.

Watching him, Porter realized that sometime over the last week, the black eye had faded completely. Cat's face was fair and perfect again, complete with the endearing freckles scattered across his nose. But something remained—a weight on those slight shoulders that was as obvious right then as if he'd still had a bruise underneath his eye.

"Hey, Champ." Porter tipped his Stetson back on his forehead. "Want to tell me what's going on?"

Cat continued raking but slowed at the words. Abby stood behind him, sniffing his jeans. Up in the rafters, pigeons cooed and shook their feathers, sending a few down like snowflakes.

Cat finally looked up. “It’s nothing.”

Porter pushed off the barn door and walked over to the stall. The sun filtered through the slats in the old roof, lighting the boy and horse in a sunbeam. Dust hung in the air like stars.

“I’m not sure I buy that,” he said.

“It’s mostly true.”

“Mostly?”

Cat shrugged. “I’ve just been thinking.”

“About?”

“My grandma…my dad.”

Porter waited for him to go on. Not wanting to push, but knowing at the same time that a little push might be exactly what he needed.

The boy leaned the rake against the stall door and turned to the little horse that had her nose in his ear. He took her head in his hands, before looking over at Porter.

“My dad must not know my grandma is sick. Otherwise, he would’ve come back.”

Porter nodded at that. Maybe he didn’t know. But the question was more complicated than that. Justine had told him the other day that Calvin had been out of the picture for years. Since Cat was practically a baby. That didn’t sound like a man who would hightail it back when he found out his kid's grandma was in poor health. But then again, maybe he would. The truth was, nobody would ever know for sure, unless they got in touch with Calvin. Until then, Cat would be left guessing. And waiting.

"I know he and my mom were really young when they had me," Cat said evenly. "I know that's one of the reasons he left. He didn't know how to be a dad. But I'm going to find him. Maybe he'll see that I'm bigger now, and it wouldn't be so scary."

Porter's heart twisted. This was an eleven-year-old's logic. A simple explanation for something that wasn't so simple. Porter had come up with these kinds of excuses for his own mother as a kid. Even going so far as making up stories as to why she'd left and hadn't come back—she was sick, she'd gotten knocked on the head and forgotten that she'd had a family, she'd been kidnapped and taken out of the country. All pretty pathetic stuff that he understood now was a boy's way of trying to come to terms with his abandonment.

Cat's thought process wasn't nearly as far-fetched, and actually, it made some sense. But that didn't mean it would pan out in the end.

"You miss your dad, don't you?" Porter asked quietly.

Cat nodded. "I have to find him."

"You have to?"

"My grandma wants me, but she's sick. She can't be raising a kid right now."

Porter ground his teeth together. The truth was a cruel, bitter pill to swallow.

"And Justine is leaving at the end of the school year," Cat continued. "She doesn't think I know, but I do. My mom died when I was two, did she tell you that?"

"She did," Porter said, trying to keep the emotion out of his voice.

"So, my mom's gone, and I really don't have anyone else. I need to find my dad, so we can start over."

Porter studied his boots for a few seconds. When he looked back up, he knew he had to say something. Someone might argue that it wasn't his place, and he guessed it wasn't. But the connection he felt to this little boy, their shared experience, had introduced some kind of responsibility that he couldn't deny.

"Cat," he said. "I know it's hard to think about, and you might not be happy with me saying it…but have you considered that maybe he still doesn't know how to be a dad?"

Cat stroked Abby's nose. "I've thought of that," he finally said. "I know if I find him, it might be weird for him. And for me, too. But I need to try."

"I get it. My mom left when I was a kid, too. I know how you feel."

Cat raised his brows. "Did you try and find her?"

"Nope. I've always been a little afraid to."

"Afraid of your mom?"

"Afraid of who she is. The picture I've painted of her isn't very nice."

"A protective mechanism."

"A what?"

"A protective mechanism. My grandma knows a lot about psychology. She helps me work stuff out. I think she's worried that I'm sad about my dad leaving, and I am. I think that's normal, right?"

Porter nodded. That was the understatement of the century.

"But I feel like I'm going to be more sad if I don't see him again."

"Even if it doesn't go how you want it to?"

"Yeah. Because at least then I'll know. Don't you want to know about your mom?"

Porter grit his teeth. He used to think he did. Now, he wasn't so sure. He was a grown man and had left a lot of that pain behind. Or at least he liked to think he had. But standing here, talking about it now, he could feel that same old emptiness yawning inside him. That place that his mother had created when she left. It had never been filled by anything else in Porter's life. Even now. Even all these years later.

"What if you tried to find her?" Cat continued, his expression hopeful. "What if you found your mom, and I found my dad, and we did it together? That way it wouldn't be so hard."

Porter hadn't thought about trying to find his mom in years. He'd mentioned it once a long time ago, but Brooks and Griffin had shrugged it off. They were all in a good place now. They had their dad, and their family felt whole. Why go ruining that by opening up old wounds?

"I don't know, Champ," he said.

"I'm just saying…maybe she's been wanting to find you, but she's just scared," Cat finished matter-of-factly.

It was as if Porter's younger self, the boy from all those moons ago, was standing here rationalizing with himself. He used to wonder the same thing over and over again…*maybe she's just scared.*

He didn't necessarily like the way those words had formed a hook, and were now pulling at his heart. His mother had left. She'd left, and that had been a conscious choice. Seeing her again wouldn't change any of that. Except, he knew that it might change how he felt about it.

Cat patted Abby's neck before reaching for the rake again. "Hey, do you think Justine can learn to ride, too?"

Porter looked down at him, relieved at the sudden change of subject. "What?"

"Well, speaking of being scared."

"She's scared of horses?"

"No, my grandma says she's scared of people, but don't tell her I told you that."

Porter filed that away under things to think more about later. Justine was scared of people? Or scared of getting close to people? There was a difference, and he wasn't sure about the former, but he sure as shit could identify with the latter.

"Scout's honor," he said, holding up two fingers.

"I bet she'd like it, though. She was telling me the other night it was something she always wanted to try, but never got around to it. And now, she's moving to London and who knows if they even *have* horses there."

"I think they probably have horses in London, Champ. But I get your point."

"I mean, she's bringing me out here after school and on the weekends anyway. Maybe she could take some lessons, too."

Actually, there was nothing Porter would like more than seeing Justine Banks on the back of a horse.

"Huh," he said, rubbing his chin. "Maybe we can arrange that."

Cat grinned. He was nothing if not convincing.

Chapter Six

JUSTINE'S PHONE DINGED, and she looked down at the text message from Nola. Her heart swelled, just like it always did when she heard from her old friend.

"Everything okay?" her dad asked.

He sat across from her at Rocco's, their favorite Italian restaurant. His thick white hair was freshly cut this afternoon, and he wore a brown Pendleton shirt with his reading glasses tucked inside the chest pocket. He usually needed them for menus, but he ordered the same thing every Sunday, so he hadn't bothered putting them on.

"Nola just wants to check in," she said. "Tell me how her appointment went on Friday."

"You said she's trying a new treatment?"

Justine nodded. It was new, and so far, it looked promising. But Nola was an eternal optimist. Sometimes it was hard getting her to admit how tired she was, or how she really felt about things.

"I'm praying for her, kiddo," he said, leaning forward to pat her hand.

"Thanks, Dad. She'd appreciate that."

A server walked by balancing a steaming pepperoni pizza, trailing the smell of warm bread and cheese behind him.

"Why don't you give her a call?" her dad said. "We can wait to order."

She looked at her watch. It was getting late, and he had a date in a few hours. A woman he'd met on a seniors' matchmaking site. They were going to the pumpkin patch. Justine was still getting used to watching her father negotiate the world as a single guy. To her, he was still connected to her late mother, something she was going to have to start untangling in her heart.

"Are you sure?" she asked. "I don't want to make you late."

"You're not going to. And even if I was, Nancy would understand."

"She sounds nice."

"She is. And she can't wait to meet you girls."

He'd mentioned it twice now. She'd have to run this by Jemma, although she knew her little sister would be completely on board with their dad having a new girlfriend. Jemma was nothing if not romantic. Justine was more worried about realistic things, like him getting taken advantage of, or getting his heart broken. *A buzzkill.* That's what Jemma called her. Whatever. She could live with that.

"Okay," she said, grabbing her phone. "I'll just be outside."

"Take your time. I'll order our drinks."

Justine wound her way around the small tables covered with red checkered cloths and pushed open the door into the chilly afternoon air. Heavy, dark clouds hung in the sky, promising rain later. She zipped her puffer jacket to her chin and stood underneath Rocco's cute little awning to call Nola.

The phone only rang once before she picked up.

"Hello?"

"Nola?"

"Justine! Hey there, toots."

Justine smiled into the collar of her jacket. "I got your text. I just wanted to call to see how you were."

"Oh, hanging in there. I'm actually feeling pretty good. Tired, but better."

"I'm so glad! By the way, I sent you some socks. They should be there by the end of the week."

"The ones with polar bears?"

"I got the last pair. I had to arm wrestle some lady for them, but you know."

Nola laughed. She'd discovered Marietta Western Wear on a visit last winter. She had Justine check in every few weeks to see what kind of socks they had in stock. Nola loved cozy socks.

"How's our little man doing?" she asked.

"Great. No more fights at school."

Nola exhaled on the other end of the line. "Good, good. That's good news."

"He loves the ranch, being around all those animals. And

he's bonded with Porter. Which, you know. Makes me a little worried."

"Not everyone is going to let him down, sweetie."

A man walked by with a fluffy golden retriever straining at his leash. He made a beeline for Justine, before his owner pulled him close.

She watched the dog wag his feathery tail at no one in particular, and sighed. "I guess having Cat here is bringing all my stuff back."

"With your dad?"

"With my dad. With my ex-boyfriends. Even with my mom. Sometimes it's just easier to stay unattached."

"But that's no way to live, Justine."

"No, it's not. Which brings me to something I've been needing to tell you…"

She buried her free hand in her pocket and hunched her shoulders in the chilly breeze. She'd been putting this off for a reason. Telling Nola about Calvin was going to open up a whole can of worms. And her friend didn't really need any more worms in her life at the moment.

"I know where Calvin is going to be in November," she finished evenly.

A few seconds went by before her friend answered. "Okay…I'm afraid to ask…."

"Marietta," Justine said. "There's a stock auction here right before Thanksgiving, and Porter heard he's planning on coming. They have rodeo friends who run in the same circle."

"Oh boy."

"Cat's been talking about his dad a lot lately, Nola. He wants to find him."

"I know he does. This was inevitable. Of course it was. I was just hoping to put it off as long as possible. So he'd be a little older, better able to handle the outcome, whatever it turns out to be."

"That makes perfect sense."

"But life has a way of throwing us curveballs, doesn't it?"

Justine frowned. *Yes, it does.*

"Well," Nola continued softly, "I'm sorry you're having to deal with this. It's enough that you've taken him in for me."

"Don't be silly. He's a joy. And I'm just happy to be able to help."

"And you are, toots. It's such a blessing having him there. I hate the thought of that little firecracker having to come back and live with his old grandma next year. Marietta is such a good place for him."

Justine swallowed hard. It wasn't just a good place for Cat, it was a great place. But she was headed overseas, and as wonderful as it was turning out to be, this arrangement would have to come to an end eventually. As usual, the thought made her stomach sink.

"Anyway," Nola continued matter-of-factly, "we'll cross that bridge when we come to it. We've got enough on our plate with this Calvin situation."

"He hasn't been in touch?" Justine asked. "Not at all?"

"Oh, I've heard from him here and there. But not for ages. I have no idea what kind of man he's grown into, but I do think his heart used to be in the right place. He was just never ready to take responsibility for anything, always bouncing from one place to the next. And there was probably a part of him that wondered if Cat was even his..."

Justine sighed.

"The rodeo suited him," Nola continued. "The danger, the nomadic lifestyle. I think that's what drew Melissa to him in the first place. She wanted to tame him, but the more she tried, the wilder he got. She never had a chance, and neither did Cat. Not really."

Justine gazed at the park across the street. And beyond that, to where the Marietta River flowed in dark, glassy currents underneath the steely sky. There was something so tragic about Cat's family story. Not just that his mom died young, but that she'd loved someone who was too wild for her. It reminded Justine of her own mom, and the fact that her dad had left, too. Different circumstances, same result. Nothing in life was guaranteed. Especially love.

She felt a sudden stinging behind her eyes. *Poor Cat.* She understood what it was like to be left behind. She understood the scars that people could inflict. Even the most well-meaning people.

"Do you want me to tell him?" she asked, her voice a little hoarse. "That his dad might be in town?"

Her friend sighed on the other end of the line. She was probably weighing the options, knowing there weren't many.

"Shoot," Nola finally said. "I think we have to. He'll find out anyway. Maybe he'll decide he doesn't need to see his daddy after all. Maybe being in Marietta will help push that other stuff to the background a little."

Justine watched the orange and red maples in the park shiver in the breeze. They looked chilly, too. She wondered if Marietta was enough to make Cat forget about his dad and all the complications there. She could only compare it to her own experience, but knew that nothing, not even pushing her dad out of her life right after he left, made the hurt go with him or ease it from her heart. It just sat there, cold and heavy, like a stone. Making her feel weary and weighted down. She could only guess what it was doing to Cat's heart, which was still small, impressionable, and growing.

"Okay," she said. "I'll tell him. Try not to worry about it, alright? I'll let you know how it goes. And in the meantime, we'll keep him busy at the ranch."

"Speaking of…you haven't told me enough about this ranch. Or the young man who runs it…"

"Porter?"

"He's a looker."

Justine laughed. "How do you know that?"

"But you're not arguing?"

"No. He's…attractive." *Understatement.*

"When you told me Cat was taking lessons, I had to google the ranch. And the owners."

Justine had forgotten about Diamond in the Rough's website. She'd looked at it before the field trip, too. And had seen the same pictures Nola had. As good as they were, they didn't do Porter justice.

"So, you've been spending time with him?" Nola asked.

"A little."

"Cat says you're out there several times a week. That's more than a little. And he came to Cat's science fair at school?"

Justine knew where this was going. Nola was always trying to marry her off. *For godchildren!* she'd say. And Justine knew there was more than a little truth to that. Over the last couple of years, they'd settled into more of a mother-daughter relationship, and that came with a fair amount of prodding where her love life was concerned.

"He's a nice guy," Justine said. "But don't get your hopes up."

"Why not? There's always hope for you."

"Ha ha."

"He's single, isn't he?"

"Yup."

"Then why can't I get my hopes up?"

"I'm leaving, remember?"

Nola snorted. "Bah. That's what airplanes are for."

Shaking her head, Justine smiled. "I love you."

"I know."

"I'll call you later tonight. Dad and I are going to grab a bite before his date."

"Joe's dating?"

"Yes, and she's nuts about him."

"Well, he's a good man."

"I'll tell him you said so."

"Don't you dare. It'll go straight to his head."

Justine laughed, then hung up and stood there under Rocco's awning as people walked by. She thought about telling Cat about his dad, and how he might react. With excitement? Nerves? Or maybe Nola was right—maybe somewhere over the last few weeks he'd gotten distracted enough with the ranch that it might be more of an interesting sidenote for him, something to explore but not to worry about. She hoped, however it went, that it wouldn't cause any more heartache. It was hard enough being eleven without throwing this into the mix.

Tucking her phone into her jacket pocket, she turned and saw her dad through Rocco's front window. He was sitting there, sipping a soda and messing with his phone. Suddenly, her heart swelled with love for him. He'd walked out on their family all those years ago, yes. But he'd spent the better part of a decade trying to make up for it. Porter had been right—their story had a happy ending. She hoped there would be a happy ending for Cat, too.

She opened the door to a blast of warm air. *Thank God*

for the ranch. And thank God for Porter Cole, who was easing Cat's way more than he probably knew.

And at the thought of the dark-haired cowboy across town, she smiled.

Her dad looked up and smiled back. "Well? How'd it go?"

Chapter Seven

PORTER STOOD WITH his arms crossed over his chest, trying his damndest not to let his gaze fall to Justine's butt, which was where it really wanted to be. Instead, he cleared his throat, and nodded when she glanced back with a look of concern on her pretty face.

"Like this?"

"Just like that."

She had one boot in the stirrup, and one hand on the back of the saddle. Bailey, Porter's old bay gelding, stood quietly with his head down and his eyes half-closed. He was used to this kind of thing—beginners swinging clumsy legs over his back, gripping big chunks of his mane to steady themselves. He was unfazed. He swished his tail lazily, and it brushed against Justine's jacket with a soft swoosh.

She pushed her knit hat up on her forehead and took a breath. "He's so big."

"He's big, but he's just going to stand there until you get settled, I promise."

Her lips tilted into a funny half-frown. "And then what?"

"He'll do what you tell him to." This, from Cat, who

was sitting on the arena fence and watching with interest. Porter suspected he liked not being the newbie anymore. With Justine getting ready to haul herself onto Bailey's back for the first time, Cat was now in a position of offering little nuggets of wisdom. Such as, *he likes it when you scratch under his chin*, or *look out, he's about to poop!*

So far, Justine had been taking all this in stride. But now that she was about to actually climb aboard, she looked stiff and nervous, her shoulders hunched up next to her ears.

"Here…" Porter walked up behind her and put his hands on her hips. He'd been avoiding this for obvious reasons, because touching her at all made his pulse react accordingly. Not exactly anything he'd want Cat to pick up on. The kid didn't miss a beat. Plus, he didn't trust that Justine wouldn't pick up on it, too. He was more than a little attracted to her and wasn't ready for all the complication that would bring. Mainly, wanting to get her into bed.

"Okay," he said, trying to ignore the feel of her curves underneath his hands. "Lift yourself up, and I'll help. Just try and swing your leg wide to clear his back."

"Easier said than done," she muttered. "I haven't been that flexible since high school."

He smiled.

Turning, she gave him a look over her shoulder. "You know what I mean."

"Sure."

"Okay. One…two…" She bounced a little, which wasn't

helping his frame of mind any. "*Three.*"

With a small grunt, she lifted herself up and swung her leg wide like he'd told her. Bailey stood there, still as a statue.

Justine settled herself on his back, as Porter handed over the reins.

"You did it," he said.

"You helped."

Actually, he wouldn't mind if they did it again. "Not much. Just kept you upright."

He gave her a teasing grin, and her cheeks colored. *Bingo.* He liked that he could get a reaction out of her so easily. He'd never really had to work that hard with women, but something about Justine was different. He wasn't sure why. He had absolutely no intention of any kind of relationship, with her or anyone else. But since he'd met her, he'd been thinking of things that he hadn't allowed himself to think of before. If ever.

She turned around and beamed at Cat, the saddle creaking underneath her. She was beautiful, but her looks were only part of the reason why Porter was so drawn to her. The way she was with this little boy also did something to him. She was a good person. A loving person. He thought of his own mother, someone who couldn't even be bothered with her own sons, let alone someone else's.

He patted Bailey's hind end, and the horse raised his head.

"Uh oh," Justine said warily.

"He's just getting ready to go to work," Porter said.

"Now that I'm up here," she said, brushing her hair away from her face, "what exactly does 'work' mean?"

"For now, it means walking in a circle, and getting used to the feel of a horse underneath you. Squeeze a little with your legs, and he'll go. That's it. Good."

"Justine, you can learn how to jump on Bailey!" Cat said. "I did it the other day and it's awesome."

"I'm not sure she's quite ready for the Olympics, Champ."

"Yeah," Justine agreed. "I'm having a hard enough time staying on at a walk, right Bailey?" She leaned down and stroked the horse's fuzzy neck.

"It's not a bad idea, though," Porter said.

Bailey kept walking, slow and steady, always the perfect gentleman.

Justine glanced over. "What's not a bad idea?"

"The jumping part. I mean, nothing big…more like an obstacle course. When you start getting more confident. It's a great way to build trust between you and your horse. A good way to bond."

"We're bonding just fine like this."

"I bet you'd be great at it, Justine," Cat said.

"I'm actually scared of horses," she said, swaying along with Bailey's easy gait.

"You don't look scared," Porter said. "You have a nice seat."

"What does that mean?"

"It means you have a good butt," Cat said matter-of-factly.

Justine fixed Porter with a smile.

"That's not exactly what it means..." *But you do have a nice butt.* "Technically, it means you have a natural way of moving in the saddle."

"Oh. Well, I'll take it, then."

"I'll bet you a cup of coffee that you'll be hooked by the end of the day."

She shifted in the saddle, looking more comfortable by the minute. Her dark hair hung in loose, shiny ringlets past her shoulders. Her cheeks were pink from the chilly afternoon air. She was lovely.

"Oh yeah?" she said. "And is this good coffee?"

"Is this *good* coffee? I'll forgive you for that, because we don't know each other very well. But everyone around here knows I'm the coffee king."

Cat hopped down from the fence. "Can I spend extra time with Abby, then?"

Justine had said that after the lesson, they were headed into town for some lunch and shopping. Apparently, Cat needed socks and underwear, an adventure that he'd been less than excited about. He looked at them now with a desperate expression on his face.

Justine glanced at Porter. "You probably have work to do..."

"Actually, we don't have any guests right now. The ranch hands have it covered. And I'm due for some coffee anyway."

"So, Abby?" Cat asked.

"A visit from you would make her day."

Cat beamed. "Can I bring Alloy some apples, too?"

He'd made a friend out of the big bull, who came over to the fence every time he saw Cat coming. The apples helped. But there was no denying Cat had a way with animals that couldn't be taught. It was a gift. Porter wondered what his father would think of it if he knew. He wondered what he would think of Cat if he knew any damn thing about him.

At that, there was a small flash of anger deep inside Porter's chest. His own mother didn't know anything about her sons, either. She should. She should know how their dad had eventually stepped in to fill the void. She should know how her boys made it without her. How they'd even managed to thrive in Montana. She should know a whole hell of a lot of things, but she didn't. Because she'd run like a coward. Just like Calvin Roberson had.

Justine pulled Bailey to a stop in front of him. The horse nudged his pockets, looking for a treat.

Reaching up, Porter rubbed his soft, whiskery muzzle. Animals had never let him down. Not once in all his time on the ranch. It was people that couldn't be trusted.

"Hey," Justine said quietly.

He grabbed hold of Bailey's bridle and looked up at her.

"Everything okay? You were somewhere else for a second."

He nodded but didn't answer. Thinking about his mom always took him away. Somewhere nobody had ever been able to follow.

JUSTINE SAT BESIDE the crackling fire with Clifford sleeping at her feet. The flames popped and hissed, sending sparks up when a log shifted in the bed of glowing embers.

She leaned back on the cushy leather couch and looked around. Porter lived in the ranch's guest house, a building almost as old as the main house itself. It was small, but nice. He'd prepared her for how plain it was, how simple, but she liked its simplicity. The hardwood floors gleamed, and the big, single-paned windows looked directly out onto the barn and the giant pines surrounding it. It almost felt like a treehouse, and again, she thought of how cozy it would be when it snowed, the ranch blanketed in white, and the fire roaring from the small stone hearth.

"Cream and sugar?" Porter called from the kitchen.

She could smell the coffee from where she sat. She loved coffee. It was her only vice, and if Porter's was as good as he said, she might need to find ways to be invited over more often.

"Please!"

She heard some cupboards closing, some glasses clinking

together, and then he appeared, looking too big for the small space of the living room.

"Here you go," he said. "Don't say I didn't warn you."

"Am I going to fall in love?" The words were out and hanging in the air before she realized what she'd said. *Nice, Justine.*

Settling in the chair across from her, he smiled at that. He'd hung his hat up when they'd come in, and his dark, silky hair had a ring around it that she kept wanting to run her hands through.

Instead, she wrapped them around the warm, chipped mug and stared down at the caramel-colored liquid, just so her eyes wouldn't betray her.

"It smells delicious," she said.

"Tastes pretty good, too."

"So, what's your secret?"

He leaned back, his long legs stretched out in front of him. His denim shirt gaped open at the throat, and she could see a few dark chest hairs peeking out. She shifted in her seat, suddenly warmer than she'd been a minute ago.

"Truthfully?" he asked.

"Truthfully."

"It's just Folgers. But I had to talk it up to get you to agree to a coffee date."

She laughed. "Well, I hate to disappoint you then, because you didn't have to talk it up. I love coffee. Any coffee."

"Good to know."

She took a sip, and the smoky flavor unfurled over her tongue. Something about the hot drink, the fire, the man—it was all doing something to her. Butterflies tickled her rib cage, and they brought with them a combination of lust and nerves that she hadn't experienced since her high school prom.

"So, is that what this is?" she asked. "A coffee date?"

"Is that what you want it to be?"

There was a sexy insinuation there that made her heart beat a little faster.

"Depends."

"On?"

"What that means."

He shrugged, looking maddeningly casual about the whole thing.

"You know I'm leaving," she continued evenly. It was blunt, and there was the chance he wasn't that interested anyway, but it needed to be said. As cute as he was, she had to snap out of this. She didn't have time to fall for someone right now. She had Cat to take care of. She had a job waiting overseas.

"I know," he said. "But not for a few months. Plenty of time to have some fun before then."

And there it is…

Justine had never been the type to just "have fun." When her father left her mother, all that carefree thinking flew right out the window. There were consequences to flings, even seemingly meaningless ones. Hearts got broken, shattered even. No, she wasn't the type to have fun, at least not the kind he was talking about. She could almost see Jemma rolling her eyes. *Don't be such a stick in the mud!*

She smiled into her coffee cup and took a sip. Then lowered it into her lap. "You don't know me very well."

"Isn't that the point? To get to know you?"

"But not like that."

"Like what?"

What was she supposed to say? *I know you might want to sleep with me, but I'm too much of a prude for that.*

"I'll just be honest…"

He watched her, his gaze sexy and knowing, and basically boring a hole right through her.

"I'm pretty focused on Cat right now," she continued, hating how that sounded. *Just* like a prude. "And my career."

His wide, expressive mouth tilted into a half smile. "I might not know you well, but I know your type."

She raised her brows.

"You don't want to get burned, and I get that. I've been there. In fact, I'm pretty comfortable saying I don't trust many people. Not with relationships, at least."

He'd seen right through her. Difficult? Maybe not. But he'd called her on her crap, and that was a little refreshing.

"You don't pull any punches, do you?" she asked.

"Nope."

"You're right. I don't want to get burned."

"Well, you have history. Your dad left."

She nodded.

"That would make anyone wary." He pointed to his chest. "Exhibit A."

Justine knew she shouldn't press about his personal life; she could hit a nerve. But at the same time, there was a bond between them that she couldn't deny. He understood the pain of a parent's abandonment. Only she'd mended her relationship with her dad. As far as she knew, Porter hadn't seen his mom in years.

"How long has it been since you've talked to her?" she asked, testing the waters.

"Since junior high."

She ran her hands down her thighs. She could still smell Bailey's musky horse scent on her jeans.

"I'm sorry," she said quietly. "I'm just curious."

"You can ask me anything."

Licking her lips, she tasted the coffee there. The sweetness and the cream. "Do you ever think about finding her?"

His eyes narrowed a little. The fire continued crackling beside them, the dog twitching, maybe chasing something in his dreams.

"I've thought about it," he finally said. "But not for a long time. Why?"

"I talked to Nola the other day. And told her Cat's dad is going to be in town for the livestock auction."

"Ahh. I was wondering how that would go. What did she

say?"

"That we should tell him. That he's getting old enough to decide for himself how he wants to move forward with his dad. If he wants to move forward at all."

Porter shook his head. "I hate to tell you, but I have a feeling he'll want to. He seems awfully invested in this."

He was right. She knew he was. Cat got a look in his eyes sometimes. A stubborn determination—a willfulness she wasn't used to seeing in someone so young.

"You know," Porter continued, "I told you I haven't thought about finding my mom in a long time. And that was true. Before I met you and Cat…"

Justine waited for him to go on. It seemed like he was looking for the right words. Or maybe the courage to say them out loud.

"The whole truth," he said, "is that I've been wondering where she is. What she's doing. I think about asking her why she left. Really. None of that, you're better off without me, crap. But why she left her kids, and how she was able to stay away our entire lives."

At that moment, with the light of the fire flickering across his face, he looked more like a teenager than a grown man who'd just made her coffee. His gaze settled somewhere over her shoulder as he retreated into his own thoughts. Maybe into his childhood memories, a place she knew haunted him.

Before she could think better of it, she reached out and

put a hand on his knee.

"For what it's worth," she said, "I think she was crazy to leave you."

He gave her a slow smile. Long, deep dimples cut into both scruffy cheeks. She really didn't think she'd seen a more handsome man in her life.

"You think so?" he asked.

"I know so."

"Maybe I'll look her up, then. Maybe it's time to put some of those ghosts to rest."

She realized her hand was still on his knee. Clearing her throat, she put it back in her lap.

His smile faded, his eyes looking darker and more serious than they'd been a minute before.

"Just so you know," he said, "when I said there was plenty of time to have fun before you left, I didn't mean sleeping together without any strings attached."

Her entire body hummed at the words. *Sleeping together…*

"Oh…I didn't…"

"I don't make a habit out of making mistakes, either," he continued. "And pursuing someone I could actually fall for would be a hell of a mistake. At least in my book."

She nodded slowly. "You don't want to settle down?"

"If settling down means trusting someone with my future? Then, no. I don't want to settle down."

"You don't think it might be different for you? Different

than it was for our parents?" It was a thought, or maybe even a wish, that she'd barely entertained over the years. But it had always been there, deep down. The hope that someday, she could have a marriage that worked. A relationship built on love and trust, and a mutual respect for one another that lasted throughout the years. A pipe dream, maybe. But it was what it was.

He leaned back, and it was as if he took his body heat with him. The fire still crackled merrily, but she was colder without him close.

"I used to think it could be different." He shrugged. "But you know. I've had a few bad relationships, people passing through my life that just reaffirmed what I've always believed. That maybe I'm not meant for that kind of thing."

She smiled. He sounded just like her. Two peas in a pod.

"What?"

"Nothing. It's just that we're more alike than I thought."

"A match made in hell."

"I wouldn't necessarily put it that way…"

Clifford stirred at their feet. After a few seconds, he got up and stretched.

"I should go check on Cat," Porter said, looking at his watch. "Make sure he's not in that bull's pen by now."

"He's obsessed."

"That's what I'm worried about."

Justine set her coffee cup down as Clifford rested his chin on her knee. She stroked his black and white head, his silky fur sliding underneath her fingertips. She hadn't had a pet in years—not since she was a kid. She missed the quiet, soulful relationship that came with having a dog.

Her heartbeat slowed with every stroke of Clifford's head. Calming her. Bringing things into focus. Suddenly, she made up her mind—she'd tell Cat today. She'd take him to the Main Street Diner, his favorite place for french fries, and she'd tell him about his dad.

And then she'd deal with the fallout.

Whatever that might be.

Chapter Eight

CAT SAT AT the old-fashioned soda counter with his feet dangling from the stool. He was too small for them to reach the bar at the bottom, but he didn't seem to mind. He just let his boots swing, sipping on his vanilla milkshake and mowing through his fries. Justine watched him. For such a little guy, he could sure put it away.

He swiveled toward her now, licking his lips. "Are you sure you don't want another one?"

She took a warm, golden fry and popped it into her mouth. *So. Good.* She wiped her hands on her napkin and took a deep breath.

"Cat," she said. "There's something I need to tell you."

His expression fell. "Is it about my grandma? Is she okay?"

"Yes, honey. She's doing great, actually. I just talked to her the other day."

"Oh, good."

"She misses you. But she's happy you're having fun at the ranch. She said she's going to FaceTime you this weekend."

He grinned. So many freckles. So many emotions in those bright blue eyes.

Things had been going so well these last few weeks, that she hated to introduce this wild card into the mix. But he needed to know. And she needed to be the one to tell him.

"You know about the big livestock auction that Marietta has every year?" she asked. "A lot of people come to town for it. People looking for animals to buy, horses and cattle at a good price."

At that, Cat perked up. He leaned forward and banged his boots against the counter. They made a hollow thud, and a man sitting a few stools down, looked over.

"Oh yeah. I've heard about that," Cat said. "I asked Porter if he could take me."

"You did?"

"He said maybe. That he might be busy that weekend, but he'll see."

A distinctive warmth unfurled inside Justine's chest. He'd been protecting Cat, she knew that. Waiting to see if she'd end up telling him about his dad. Being his guardian felt lonely sometimes, especially when she wondered if she was doing or saying the right thing. But knowing that Porter was in sync with her on this, even in some small way, was comforting.

"Why?" Cat asked. "Did he ask if I could go? Is he going to get a new horse or something?"

His eyes were sparkling now. Diamond in the Rough had

woken something up inside him. Deep down, he was a cowboy in the making.

"Here's the thing, honey. Porter knows a lot of people who rodeo…"

Cat stared at her. And the look on his face broke her heart in two. The hope there. The vulnerability.

She took a breath and plowed ahead. "And he's heard your dad might be planning on coming to Marietta for the auction. Right before Thanksgiving."

Cat sat completely still, letting his gaze fall to the Formica countertop. The sound of the diner buzzed around them—utensils clinking together, the low hum of people talking, the occasional burst of laughter, the door opening with the ding of a bell…

"Hey," she said softly.

He looked up at her.

"What's going on in there?"

Shrugging, he reached for his milkshake. Finally, he gave her a small smile. "Does this mean I'll get to see him?"

"It means you can try. But sweetheart, I'm not sure how that'll go. He's not expecting it, and he's been kind of off the grid for a while now…"

A woman with "Flo" printed on her nametag stopped and tapped Cat's milkshake with a red fingernail. "That's looking low. You folks let me know if you need a refill."

"Thanks so much," Justine said.

She sauntered away, tucking a pen behind her ear.

Cat watched her go, then turned back to Justine again. "Does my grandma know?"

"She does. She's worried about you, but she also thinks you're old enough to make your own decisions about your dad."

"He's been gone a while."

"Yes, he has."

"But maybe he's ready now. To be a dad."

She stayed quiet at that, her heart breaking a little more by the minute. She hoped, for his sake, that Calvin Roberson would be ready at some point soon. Because he was missing out on the most incredible boy.

"I know you're worried, too," he said. "And I promise it'll be okay. I can handle it."

He was trying so hard to be strong, to be grown-up. She reached out and squeezed his hand. His fingers were cold from holding onto the milkshake. Like ice.

"I want to see him," Cat continued. "I want to go to the auction. At least then I'll know…"

He let the words trail off, but she knew what he meant. *At least I'll know if he cares, if I mean anything to him at all…* It was a familiar question. One that she herself had chosen to leave unanswered for a long time, only to have it eat away at her heart over the years. She didn't want that to happen to Cat.

"Okay, then," she said. "If you want to go, we'll make it happen."

"Thanks, Justine."

She had no clue if this was a good idea or not. Maybe they were making a huge mistake. But it was done, and the only thing now was to lean into it. Hope that it would work out the way it was supposed to.

"I think maybe Porter wants to find his mom, too," Cat said, swirling his straw around. "Wouldn't it be great if he found his mom, and I found my dad?"

Justine's phone rang from her purse before she could reply to that. Digging it out, she saw Porter's name on the screen. His ears must've been burning.

"Hello?"

She looked over at Cat, who was looking back curiously.

"Abby's in labor," Porter said through the crackly line. She could tell he was outside—the wind blowing into the receiver. "How would you and Cat like to see a baby horse being born?"

ABBY TURNED IN a circle in the knee-deep straw, her dark brown coat shining underneath the soft yellow lighting. It was getting dark outside. The sky was grainy, and the temperature had dropped, but the old barn was still warm and cozy. It wouldn't be for long, though. A storm front was moving in, and some early snow was in the forecast. Porter was glad the little horse had gone into labor when she did.

He wanted the foal here safely before any other excitement came their way.

Stepping out of her stall now, he latched the gate behind him.

Cat stood on an old stool and peered inside. Justine stood beside him, a worried expression on her face. Apparently, this was her first time witnessing a live birth, and she kept chewing on her lip. He wasn't going to lie—that part had him inconveniently distracted.

"So, she just does it on her own?" Cat asked, looking over at him from underneath his knit cap. "You don't help?"

"I'll help if I need to," he said. "Right now, I want to give her some space. When we see the legs, I'll call Brooks. But you'll be surprised. Animals don't usually need as much help as we like to think."

"Poor thing," Justine said. "Too bad she can't have an epidural."

Porter glanced over at Abby. She did look uncomfortable as hell, but everything seemed normal so far, and was moving along at the right speed.

The horse lowered her head and sniffed the hay, looking like she was about to drop to her knees, then decided against it and turned in a circle again.

"What happens if she doesn't take to the baby?" Cat asked, his voice so low, Porter barely heard him.

"What do you mean? What happens if she were to reject it?"

Cat nodded, resting his chin on his hands.

It was obvious where that question had come from, and Porter frowned, wanting to give the kid a hug. Despite his big speech about animals knowing how to do this motherhood thing, sometimes nature didn't cooperate. Sometimes a baby was rejected, and its life started out in a very precarious spot. Those babies were sometimes raised by humans, sometimes raised by a surrogate, or by another species altogether. Cat had no doubt seen the Dodo videos of kittens being nursed by a dog, or baby squirrels being nurtured by a cat. It was interesting. The mothering instinct could be so strong, that it literally defied logic. Or it could be nonexistent. Which also defied logic. Nature was a strange business.

"It can happen," Porter said, leaning against the gate and looking in at Abby. "But when it does, other moms step up to take care of the baby. Or people do. It's hard, and it takes some adjustment, but it's the love and care that really counts." *Same goes with human babies, Champ*, he wanted to say, but didn't.

Justine caught Porter's eye then and mouthed *thank you.*

He winked at her. He'd rather promise Cat that everything would work out great with Abby's baby, but of course, he couldn't. Things happened. And as young as Cat was, it was clear that he understood this perfectly. He knew, even at the age of eleven, that life was messy.

"I run into town for some feed and look what I miss."

They all turned at the sound of the voice behind them.

Brooks stood there, his black Stetson pushed high on his forehead. His old Carhartt jacket was spotted with rain. The storm was getting closer.

"How's she doing?" he asked, stepping up to the stall to take a look.

"So far, so good," Porter said.

The horse lowered her head and swung it from side to side.

"I'd say she's getting close," Brooks said. "Not too much longer now. Who could use some coffee?"

"Me!" Cat shot his hand in the air.

"Nice try, son. We've got some hot chocolate with your name on it, though."

"I can help carry it out," Justine said. "I need to run to the bathroom anyway."

Porter looked over at her. "You sure you don't have anywhere to be? Anything else to do?"

"Not a thing. And I don't think I could drag Cat away even if we did."

Cat grinned. He was in his element. Enjoying every second. Again, Porter thought of Calvin Roberson. He should be the one teaching his son about horses having their foals. About how a ranch worked. About how to be a man, and not just that, how to be a *good* man. Cat deserved all those things.

Abby finally dropped to her knees in the straw and rolled over with a groan. Outside, the wind picked up, pushing against the barn in grumpy gusts.

"Actually, I'd wait on that coffee," Porter said, opening the stall gate. "If you don't want to miss the show."

Chapter Nine

JUSTINE PULLED HER little hatchback up to the ranch house and cut the engine. A midnight rain had started on the way back from her house, coming in sheets over Marietta.

She sat there with it drumming on the roof of the car and looked over at the barn where a warm light spilled out the door. The foal had come a few hours ago, a lovely black colt to match his mama, only he had a bold white blaze running down his face. He was beautiful and healthy, and Cat was absolutely in love.

She smiled at the memory of the birth, still fresh behind her eyes. It hadn't taken the baby long to get his wobbly legs underneath him, and they'd all watched in wonder as he took his first tentative steps in the straw, with Abby nudging him from behind.

Brooks had given Cat naming rights, which had been like a Christmas and birthday present rolled into one. And when Cat had asked if he could stay the night in the barn with Abby and her foal, Justine had looked over at Porter helplessly. She had no idea how to say no to him, his eyes shining in wonder for this little creature.

Luckily, Porter was on the same page and had pulled her aside while Cat was busy running names by Brooks.

"I used to sleep outside all the time when I was his age," he'd said, shrugging his broad shoulders. "If you're okay with it, you can stay in one of the guest rooms in the main house. They're all made up; you can take your pick. And Cat will have an adventure he'll never forget, I promise."

She'd frowned as the wind moaned around the barn. "But the weather?"

"I have a down sleeping bag, and Clifford will curl up with him. He'll keep him nice and toasty."

Justine had looked over at Cat, who was watching the foal nurse with greedy little head buts. She honestly hadn't seen him this happy in ages. There was something about tonight, about this new life coming into the world, that had touched him deeply. He felt part of the magic, and Porter was right. He would remember it forever.

"Okay," she'd said quietly. "I'll just run back to my place and get some clothes and things. He'll need some long johns and thicker socks."

Porter had smiled down at her. "You take good care of him."

The compliment felt good. Her heart seemed to have stretched to twice its size since Cat had come to stay with her. Her neat and tidy house was more cluttered now—noisier, smaller, all things that had thrown her stiff routine and structure right out the window. But they were things that she'd come to love. She liked having someone to take care of. She liked having someone to fuss over.

Porter watched her, and for a second, everything else seemed to fall away. The horses and their sweet, comforting smell. Brooks and Cat, sipping on their hot drinks and talking about names. The storm brewing outside, a reminder that fall was in full swing, and winter would follow. And that soon, she was going to be leaving all this behind.

"Justine, how about Wookiee?"

She'd glanced over at Cat. He was going through a *Star Wars* phase, as all eleven-year-olds should, in her opinion.

"I like it, buddy."

"So," Porter said. "It's a sleepover, then."

Justine sat in her car now, remembering how the words had made her heart flutter. So casual, so innocent. Yet packed with meaning.

She reached for the two small bags she'd brought for her and Cat. *A sleepover, indeed...*

The wind pushed against her little car as she zipped her jacket up to her chin. But before she could open the door, Porter appeared. Dark, hatless in the rain. With his own jacket collar pulled high.

He opened her door. "Here, hand me those," he said, nodding toward the bags. "Ready to make a run for it?"

She grabbed his free hand, and he helped her out of the car.

"Ready!"

They took off, jostling against each other and splashing in every puddle along the way. When they got to the porch, they were laughing so hard, Justine's stomach hurt. She was soaked, and so was he.

They clomped up the old steps, breathless. Porter ruffled a hand through his hair and water droplets went flying.

"You might need a towel," he said, eyeing her with a boyish grin.

"Maybe just a little one."

Inside, the house was nice and warm. It smelled like woodsmoke and bacon, and even though it was ten o'clock at night, Justine's mouth watered. Brooks had brought out sandwiches to the barn earlier, but she'd been too excited to eat. Now, she wished she had.

Porter set the bags by the door. "If you give me your coat, I'll hang it by the fire."

"Oh, I should probably run that bag out to Cat first."

"I'll do that. I'll get him all set up, but honestly, he's pretty comfortable as it is. Clifford is happy to have his very own boy for the night. So is Abby, I think. She likes the company."

"Oh, good. He might have to use the bathroom, though…"

"He came up here while you were gone. Even brushed his teeth. We keep lots of toiletries for guests, so he was good to go. I just hope he actually gets some sleep."

She shrugged off her jacket and handed it to him. Her hair hung in damp, ropy strands next to her face, and she pushed it behind her shoulder. "This is really sweet of you, Porter. To have us over like this. I think you made Cat's entire year."

"He's a great kid. Actually, he's an extraordinary kid."

She walked over to the fireplace and held her hands out to warm them. "I told him about his dad today…that he might be in town soon."

"Oh yeah?" Frowning, Porter hung her jacket up. "And how did that go?"

"Okay, I guess. He wants to see him. No surprise there."

"Maybe he won't even show up. What then?"

"We'll just have to take it as it comes. But I'm relieved that he knows. He'll be twelve soon. Almost a teenager. Nola's right. It should be his choice."

Porter stepped closer, the firelight playing over his face. "And how's Nola?"

"She's doing pretty well, actually. But she's worn out. I worry about Cat going back to her. I worry about both of them."

"I know you do. Because you're a good person."

She looked down at the popping flames. "I'm just doing what anyone would."

He chuckled softly. "Are you kidding? You're doing what *nobody* I know would do. At least that they'd do well. You're basically a foster mom. And I'm here to tell you, when you're

Cat's age and you don't have a mother, or a dad who's around…it's hard."

"But you had your aunt, right?"

"I did. And she was great. Took really good care of us. But she was busy with her own life. She cared about us, but there wasn't a ton of time for nurturing three boys."

Justine nodded. Having Cat was a joy, but she couldn't imagine having two more just like him. Exhausting wasn't a strong enough word. By the time she taught all day, then got home to make dinner and supervise homework, showered, did some chores…she practically fell into bed every night.

They stood there for a minute, silence settling between them. The fire crackled, its warmth pulsing against Justine's cheeks. It was strange how comfortable she felt in this house, with this man. It was like something had been missing for her all this time, and when she met Porter, things just fell into place. She hadn't been expecting that. She hadn't expected any of it.

He reached out and touched one of her curls that was almost dry from the heat of the fire.

"Looks like you don't need that towel after all."

Gazing up at him, she took a deep breath. She thought she could smell the faint scent of his shaving cream, although it looked like he hadn't bothered with a razor that morning. Even in the dim light of the room, she could make out the individual points of dark stubble on his chin, and she immediately imagined how that scruff would feel against her skin.

Her hands began trembling at her sides. This was what he did to her. She wondered if he felt the same tremors, the same heat in his veins.

As if answering her, he stepped closer. So close that his jacket rubbed up against her sweater. He'd unzipped it when they'd come inside, and her gaze dropped to his blue plaid shirt that gaped open at his throat. It seemed to be drawn there, to that spot where she knew she'd be able to feel his pulse tap underneath her lips.

"Hey." He put two fingers underneath her chin and lifted it until her eyes met his. "What are you thinking?"

She swallowed hard. *What am I thinking?* That she'd like to kiss him. That it had been so long since she'd met a really nice guy, that she'd forgotten what they looked like. That there was zero hope of this actually going anywhere, because she was leaving the country in just a few short months. It would be over before it could even get started.

"I'm thinking…"

He watched her, his gaze dropping to her mouth.

"I'm thinking that this isn't such a good idea," she finished softly.

He nodded but remained quiet. The firelight danced in his eyes, making them look like they were burning.

"I mean—"

"I know," he said, his voice husky. "I know you want to be careful, that you're leaving, all those things. I want to be careful, too. But I also want to kiss you, and I think you might want to be kissed."

It was probably written all over her face. She couldn't help it. And maybe she didn't *want* to help it, either.

Before she could say anything else, he leaned close. He was so tall, that she had to tilt her head all the way back to see into his eyes. And at that moment, all she could do was fall into them. Into their dark, flickering depths, where she'd been drawn since that very first day.

"Do you want to be kissed, Justine?"

She tried to answer, but her voice wouldn't cooperate. She was afraid of what she would say. So instead, she just nodded.

At that, he leaned the rest of the way in and pressed his lips to hers. So gently, that at first, they felt like butterfly wings, moving against her mouth. He didn't want to spook her, she knew that. He was taking it slow, giving her the space she needed to decide what it was she really wanted.

The thought that she was in control of this big, strong man, electrified her. She knew if she told him to stop, he would. She knew if she began unbuttoning his shirt, he'd probably let her. It electrified her. And it also scared her to death.

But instead of breaking the kiss and backing away like she absolutely knew she should, she reached up and wrapped her arms around his neck.

With a sound deep in his throat, he pulled her closer.

She felt his belt buckle press against her hip, felt her blood rush in her ears. How many women had he kissed just like this? How many hearts had he broken in his lifetime? Because at the end of the day, that's what Porter Cole was—a heartbreaker. Would he break her heart, too? She really couldn't imagine any other outcome, since the thought of leaving him tonight, or six months from now, made the backs of her eyes sting and her stomach knot almost painfully. They were playing with fire. She knew it, and he had to know it, too.

At that, she finally pulled away. He was so handsome that she had to blink a few times to clear her head. It was swimming with desire, with longing, her knees still trembling from the kiss. She was in deep. Very, very deep, and the realization was growing stronger with every ragged breath she took.

He reached up and cupped her face in both hands, running his thumbs across her cheeks. "I'm not gonna lie," he said, his voice low. "I've been wanting to do that forever."

She wasn't going to tell him how much she'd been wanting it, too. She was going to regain her composure and protect what was left of her heart. Only, even as she thought it, she couldn't help but close her eyes at the feel of his calloused fingers against her skin. He touched her like she was made of glass, like she was beautiful and something to cherish. She'd never been touched like this before. She certainly hadn't felt like this before.

She opened her eyes again and gazed up at him, so many thoughts tumbling around in her head, that she was having trouble catching just one.

"Say something, honey," he said quietly.

And the fact that he'd just called her that, made her want to cry.

She shook her head, looking over at the fire for a few seconds until the ache in her throat had eased. When she looked back, her eyes felt bright, glassy.

"When my dad left," she said, "it planted a seed in me."

He nodded, watching her, his eyes mirroring the expression on her face. Somber, quiet.

"I've let that seed grow over the years," she continued. "I've nurtured it by not trusting people, by keeping myself guarded and alone..."

She let her voice trail off then.

"You don't have to explain." He reached for her hand. Squeezing it gently, he ran his thumb over her knuckles. "I have the same seed in me. Maybe I've had more relationships than you; maybe I've jumped into bed with more people. But I'm shit when it comes to opening up. Because people leave, right? They always leave."

She gazed up at him. Loving him right then, and knowing that was ridiculous, because people didn't fall in love this easy. But the feeling was as real as anything she'd ever experienced, and at that moment, she wasn't up to fighting it. She just wanted to let it wash over her, like a warm, sparkling wave.

"Do you think you'll try and find your mom?" she asked.

He was quiet, and for a second, she worried that she'd broken the spell. That he'd shut down, and she'd shut down, too. Because that was the safest thing to do. The smartest thing.

But then he nodded. "I might," he said. "And I never thought I'd say that."

"I never thought I'd end up in Marietta, either. There was a time when I didn't think I'd ever want to see my dad again. But here I am." She smiled up at him. "I'm probably the last person who should be giving advice on forgiveness, because I still have a long way to go. But letting my dad back into my life was one of the best things I ever did."

"You think it'd be like that for me…"

"I'm not sure. But I do know if you try and find her, you shouldn't do it for her. Or even for the chance of a relationship with her. You should do it for you, Porter."

He nodded, and they were quiet. Each lost in their own thoughts.

"Hey," he said, suddenly. "It's been a long night. Are you hungry?"

She was *starving*. And was now convinced he could read her mind. Which was dangerous.

"Actually," she said, "I am."

"Me, too. There's some leftover brick oven pizza in the fridge. One of Daisy's specialties. Do you like pepperoni?"

"I *love* pepperoni."

He reached up and brushed her hair away from her face. It was the kind of thing a lover did. A boyfriend did. And before Justine could rein her heart in, it swelled.

"Why don't you sit down and get comfortable?" he said. "I'll run Cat's things out to him and make sure he's okay. Check on Abby and the foal. Then I'll warm up some pizza for us and we can have a glass of wine by the fire. Sound good?"

Justine didn't trust herself to speak. Her emotions were running too high, and she was falling too fast. Instead, she nodded, biting the inside of her cheek.

"Okay. Be right back."

She watched him head to the door, and open it into the grumpy storm. And then he was gone, disappearing into the autumn night like a ghost.

Looking over at the fire, she sank down onto the couch and ran her fingertips over her lips. They were still tingling. She could still smell his warm, spicy scent on her hands, could still feel him against her skin.

She sighed. Then leaned back against the soft, leather cushions, and decided to enjoy the moment.

Even if it wouldn't last.

Chapter Ten

PORTER PULLED HIS truck up to the curb in front of Mistletoe Music, his dad's shop, and cut the engine. The rain had stopped an hour ago, and the sun had poked its head out of the clouds, making Main Street shine like a black, sequined dress.

Cat unbuckled his seat belt and looked out the window. He was excited. Even though the height of Eddie Cole's fame had been way before Cat's time, he was still a household name, and kids Cat's age had been introduced to him through the magic of YouTube and TikTok videos. So he was a big deal. Especially in Marietta.

Looking over at Porter, Cat grinned. He was smiling more lately, some of the weight on his slight shoulders seeming to ease over the last few weeks. "I like not being in school on a weekday," he said. "It's sick."

Porter was still getting acquainted with the middle school lingo. The first time Cat had said something was sick, he'd actually asked what he meant. *Is that good or bad?* Then he felt eighty years old.

He unbuckled his own seat belt and opened the truck

door. "Pretty sick."

It was Monday, but it was a teacher in-service day, so all the kids were out of school. Justine was behind on grading and had asked if Cat could spend the day at the ranch.

As she'd driven away that morning, and he'd watched her go with his heart in his throat, Cat had asked what they were going to do.

He'd looked down and ruffled his red hair. "Well, a few guests are coming in this morning and I'll need to get them checked in. But after that, Brooks is gonna take over. Which means we've got the day to ourselves. What sounds good, Champ?"

"Can we go to Eddie's shop?"

This hadn't surprised him much. Cat had been wanting to meet his dad for a while, and it was the perfect day for it. "You got it. But be prepared, he's a character. And he dresses weird."

Cat had laughed, clearly encouraged by this.

They both stepped onto the sidewalk now, the chilly breeze snatching at their jackets. Porter jammed his Stetson down lower on his head and looked over when Cat groaned beside him.

"What?"

Cat didn't answer, just stared straight ahead.

Porter followed his gaze to a group of girls heading toward them. Giggling, holding their drinks, peering into the shop windows. They looked to be Cat's age, but it was hard to tell since they were so bundled up.

He looked back at Cat. "You know them?"

"They go to my school." The look on his face suggested he might like one of them. His freckled cheeks were flushed red. From the cold maybe. But maybe from something else, too.

The girls got closer and Porter clamped his mouth shut, determined not to butt in. Even though what he really wanted was to poke the kid in the ribs and tell him to say hello.

Cat stopped on the sidewalk and bent to tie his shoelace that was already tied. His small back was hunched, his head down in an obvious attempt not to be seen.

It didn't work.

"Cat?"

One of the girls stopped right in front of him, smiling wide, her braces flashing in the sun. She wore a long, blond braid over one shoulder, and a purple knit hat with a pom-pom on top. She was adorable.

Porter smiled down at her, then looked over at Cat, willing him to stand up and say something. Anything.

Instead, he stared up at her with his mouth hanging open. This was not the precocious kid Porter was used to seeing at the ranch. The fearless one with all the witty one-liners. This kid looked like he wanted the sidewalk to open up and swallow him whole.

The other two girls laughed softly and whispered something to each other.

"I'm Amber," the blonde said, looking up at Porter. "Cat's in my class."

"Nice to meet you, Amber. Girls."

The other two smiled back but were already looking bored. Adults were obviously a buzzkill.

Cat recovered enough to stand up.

"Hi," he said. His voice, which had a tendency to crack, didn't today, thank God.

Amber smiled wide, ignoring her friends. Porter was no expert, but it seemed like she might like him, too.

"Are you getting ready for Thanksgiving?" she asked. "My aunt and uncle are flying in from New Orleans. We always make gumbo for them. It's pretty good."

Porter watched Cat closely. This poor kid didn't have family coming in from anywhere. His Thanksgiving would be small, most likely with Justine, her dad and sister. It was his reality, so different from the little girl standing in front of him, probably loved beyond measure and spoiled rotten.

Cat nodded. "My dad…he might be coming to have dinner with us."

Well, shit. Porter hadn't expected that. And he had no idea if Cat actually believed it, or if he was just saying it to feel included. Either way, it broke his heart a little.

"That's cool," she said.

Amber's friends tugged on her jacket sleeve. They were ready to go.

"Well..." Cat buried his hands in his pockets. "I'll see you in school."

"See you in school."

They walked off, but she waved before they disappeared around the corner.

Staring after her, Cat frowned. "Don't say it."

"Don't say what?"

"I don't like her or anything."

"Okay. But she seems to like you."

Cat looked up at him. "She does?"

"Just saying... And it's okay to like her, you know. If you do."

"Everybody likes her. Alec James likes her."

"Who's Alec James?"

"That kid from the field trip that day."

Porter sighed inwardly. Ahh. *That* Alec James.

"Besides," Cat went on. "She's nice to everyone. It doesn't mean anything."

He seemed grumpy now, surly. Amber was obviously a sore subject. Porter could relate. He was still trying to figure out what he and Justine were to each other.

"I know my dad might not come for Thanksgiving," Cat said. "But if I find him, maybe I can ask?"

Porter put a hand on his shoulder. "I think if you asked, and Justine said it's okay, he'd be crazy not to come, Champ."

This got a small smile. Not huge, but it was something.

"Come on," Porter said. "Let's go. My dad's excited to meet you."

"He is?"

"He absolutely is. In fact, he asked if I thought you might want to play his guitar a little. You know. To test it out."

Eddie Cole had a lime-green electric guitar that was almost as famous as he was. He'd played it in one of his most iconic music videos. Everyone knew the lime-green guitar from *Mistletoe Magic*.

Cat's face lit up.

"So, you'd like that?" At this point, it was a rhetorical question, but what the hell.

"Uh, *yeah*."

"Okay, then. Let's get after it."

A minute later, Porter was holding the shop door open for Cat. The boy walked through, looking like he'd just arrived at Disneyland. There were glossy instruments everywhere. Customers with stars in their eyes. Shiny platinum albums hanging on the historic brick walls. Even an MTV Video Music Award in a shadow box above the staircase, Eddie Cole's pride and joy.

It was all here. All the evidence of a life well lived, of a career sprinkled with more than a little magic dust, and some good old-fashioned luck thrown in for good measure.

Eddie was a product of his time, a product of his rock and roll lifestyle, and when he walked gracefully down the stairs in tight leather pants and a leopard print shirt opened to his sternum, Porter had to smile.

"Is this who I think it is?" he asked, grinning down at Cat, his teeth flashing white against tanned skin.

Cat smiled back. All the shyness from his encounter with Amber gone, he stepped forward and stuck out his hand.

Now, *this* was the kid Porter knew so well. Standing back, he watched with his thumbs hooked in his belt loops, feeling good that he could make this happen. Not every kid got to meet a rock icon at eleven years old. And for a second, he saw his dad through Cat's eyes. How cool this must be to shake the hand of one of the most talented guitarists from the second half of this century. At least, Porter thought so.

"You must be Cat," his dad said. "It's a pleasure."

"Hello, Mr. Cole."

Porter felt a swell of pride at Cat's manners. Old-fashioned, polite. His grandmother had done a great job with him. And he knew Justine was trying to nurture those things, too.

"You know what they say about Mr. Cole," his father said. "That's my dad. Call me Eddie."

"Okay, Eddie. I have all your albums."

"Oh yeah?"

"*Rock and a Hard Place* is my favorite."

Porter's dad looked genuinely surprised. It was his favorite, too, but his fans usually liked *Mistletoe Magic* the best. Which was definitely his most popular.

"A true Eddie Cole connoisseur, I see."

Cat blushed, obviously happy with the compliment.

"Porter tells me you're taking lessons at the ranch."

"Yup."

"And you named a baby horse the other night? Tell me about that."

Porter listened as Cat launched into the subject of names, listing all the ones he'd considered before settling on Wookiee.

"It fit the best," Cat said. "Even though he's black and he reminded me of Darth Vader at first."

"That's a solid name, son."

"Porter says he's gonna be big, like his dad. He's got really long legs and he's not afraid of anything. He should be good around cattle. That's what Brooks said."

"Huh. You know, Porter tried to get me on a horse a few weeks ago, and I fell flat on my ass."

"Dad…"

"Sorry." His dad slapped his leather-clad rear end. "Not much padding here. Couldn't walk straight for two days."

Cat laughed.

"Anyway, thought you might like to play some guitars in the back. Maybe strum the old Green Goblin. Would you like that?"

"Yes!"

"See that guy over there with the mohawk?" Porter's dad pointed to an employee showing a woman a drum set.

"That's Kody. He's going to show you around the shop for a few minutes, and then I'll come back there and jam with you, okay?"

Cat nodded, looking thrilled.

"Alright then."

Kody looked up as Cat approached and gave him a fist bump.

"I like that kid," his dad said, crossing his arms over his skinny chest. "I knew I would. I think he's a born musician."

Porter laughed. "You've known him for like five minutes."

"Doesn't matter. I can tell."

"Well, don't get too excited. He wants to ride bulls like his dad."

They watched as Kody handed Cat a glossy, honey-colored ukulele off the wall.

"His old man, huh?" Porter's dad said, leaning against the staircase. "Didn't you say he was going to be in Marietta soon?"

"That's what I heard."

"Do you think he'll see Cat?"

"I don't even think he knows he's here. He hasn't been in touch with Cat's grandma for a while."

"And she's the one raising him?"

Porter nodded.

"What a shitshow."

Kody led Cat off to where the electric guitars hung in the

back. The coolest part of the shop, as far as Porter was concerned.

"You know," his dad said, clasping his hands in front of his snakeskin belt, "he reminds me a lot of you at that age."

Porter raised his brows.

"Yeah," he continued. "Believe it."

"How?"

"Precocious, smart, sensitive…"

"I was never that sensitive."

"You were. More than your brothers. I worried about that when I sent you here. Actually, I worried about that most of all."

It had been a hard time in Porter's childhood, but his dad had made the right decision. He'd been a single father who just couldn't handle raising three boys on his own at that point in his life, and he'd known it. Giving his sons the gift of a Montana childhood had made them who they were today. Porter would always be grateful for that.

He reached out and touched his dad's elbow. "But it turned out okay, didn't it?"

"It did. Marietta was the right place for you boys. And it looks like it's the right place for this kid, too. I just hope his old man doesn't screw it up."

Porter looked over at Cat who was now holding a cherry-red Gibson, looking like he'd won the middle schooler lottery.

"Maybe if he sees Cat, he'll come around."

His dad shook his shaggy blond head. "I wasn't a great father, but I can't imagine writing my kid off like that."

"Me neither. And by the way, you were a good dad. It was Mom who was shit at the parenting thing."

His father stayed quiet at that. If the memory of sending Porter and his brothers to Marietta was a sensitive subject, then the one of their mother leaving was like walking on a sidewalk full of eggshells while wearing combat boots.

"Dad..."

He looked over.

Porter grit his teeth for a second, trying to decide if he should say what he'd been thinking these last few days. The look on his father's face was guarded. Maybe he already knew. His dad had always been weirdly intuitive when it came to his sons. Even when he used to live two thousand miles away from them.

"What would you say if I told you I was thinking about trying to find her?"

His dad watched him. Then let out a low breath. The shop seemed to grow quiet. Even Cat had stopped strumming the guitar in the back room.

Porter knew his dad had worked hard to put his ex-wife's memory to rest. She'd abandoned them all, and at the time, he'd still loved her very much. Yeah, they'd had their problems. Plenty. But love had never been one of them.

He studied his dad now and wondered if he should've said anything. But at the same time, he felt like he owed it to him. Finding his mom after all this time, and not telling his father, would be like a slap in the face. It was all pretty screwed up anyway, he thought, no matter how he sliced it. Someone would probably get hurt.

But sometime over the last few weeks, the desire to see her had grown and grown, until he couldn't deny it anymore. And maybe that was because he was genuinely curious. Or maybe he needed to confront her, or know that she was doing okay. Maybe it was a combination of all of those things. And right then, more than ever, he knew exactly how Cat felt.

His dad looked down at the hardwood floor for a minute, before looking back up at Porter. His eyes were somber. "I don't know, son. I'm not sure she wants to be found."

"I know. I've thought of that."

"Can I ask you why?" he said. "After all this time?"

Porter nodded toward Cat.

His dad sighed. "Of course. Of course that's it."

"It's not all of it. But watching him go through this has stirred some things up for me."

"Well, it would. Have you talked to your brothers about this?"

"No, but I will. I wanted to run it by you first."

"And what if I told you not to do it?"

Porter rubbed the back of his neck. "Is that what you're saying?"

"No. I don't know what I'm saying."

A distinct silence fell over them. A diesel truck lumbered down Main Street and shook the single-paned windows. People stopped on the sidewalk and peered inside at the instruments, their breath fogging up the glass. Cat began strumming another guitar from across the shop, but everything still felt delicate and quiet.

Porter felt his shoulders stiffen. "I don't know… I thought I'd come to terms with her leaving a long time ago. But I haven't. I'm still pissed. More than pissed, I'm…" He found he couldn't even finish the sentence, because he didn't know *what* he was.

His dad gave him a small, rueful smile. "You don't have to explain."

"I guess I want her to know some things. I'm not sure if I'll really be able to put her behind me until I do this."

"Is that what you want? To put her behind you?"

Porter shrugged.

"Or are you hoping for some kind of relationship with her?"

And there it was. The one-million-dollar question. If someone had asked him that a month ago, he would've said hell no. But now, watching Cat navigate the unknown toward his own father, he had to admit, there was a part of him that wondered what it would be like having both parents in his life again.

"I'm not sure," he said. "I'm really not."

His dad shook his head, the diamond studs glittering in his earlobes. "It doesn't matter. It sounds like you need to do this, regardless. And I'll support you, no matter how it turns out."

Porter looked over at Cat, who had his head bent over the guitar in his lap. He was too short for the stool he was sitting on. By a lot.

"Thanks, Dad," he said, his voice low.

He had no idea how it would turn out. For him, or for Cat. But the wheels were set in motion for both of them.

Nothing to do now but sit back and hold on tight.

Chapter Eleven

JUSTINE SAT BACK in her chair at the ranch house's big dining room table and looked around at the group of guests who'd just finished their dessert. Everyone was laughing, talking in low tones, as the fire crackled from the other room. It was a dusky, cold Sunday evening, with stars beginning to sparkle outside the foggy windows.

"Coffee, hon?"

She glanced up at Daisy and smiled. "No, thank you. I'm stuffed. I can't even sip on anything else."

"I know the feeling, but you get used to it. Meals are kind of a big deal out here."

She let her gaze settle on Porter, who was showing Cat how to make a bird out of his folded napkin. When he'd called that morning to invite them to dinner, she'd made an apple pie, her favorite. Everyone seemed to have liked it, cleaning their plates and asking for seconds. This made her happy, since she loved baking. And as she watched Cat lick some whipped cream off his finger, she vowed to do it more often. It was good for her heart.

Porter looked up. They'd been watching each other all

evening, an electricity sparking between them that Justine was surprised wasn't visible to the naked eye.

Some of the guests began getting up and taking their coffees into the living room to drink by the fire. Apparently, it was going to be an early morning with a trail ride down by the river, so some of them were talking about heading to bed soon.

Cat got up and came around to her side of the table.

"Can I go out to the barn to see Abby and Wookiee?"

"If Porter says it's okay," she said. "But don't forget your hat and gloves, alright?"

"Okay."

Porter looked up at Daisy as she cleared his dessert plate. "Can I help with dishes?"

"Oh," Justine said, "me, too. I'd love to help."

"No, I'm fine. Brooks is going to help, aren't you, Brooks?"

"Sure. I love doing dishes with you, babe."

Daisy gave him some side-eye, before glancing back at Porter and Justine. "Why don't you two go for a walk? It's such a gorgeous night."

"She's trying to get us alone together," Porter said dryly.

"I am not."

Brooks laughed. "Just admit it. You're matchmaking again. And not being very subtle at it, either."

"Okay. Maybe a little."

They all looked at her.

"Okay. A *lot.* But can you blame me? Somebody has to move this along. If we left it up to you two, it'd take forever."

Warmth flooded Justine's cheeks. It was true. All of it. Since their kiss, she and Porter had been dancing around each other for days. Sneaking glances, looking away, looking back again. She'd told him she wasn't in the market for any kind of relationship, and he'd agreed that he wasn't, either. But they couldn't seem to move on from that kiss, no matter how hard they tried. And let's face it, they hadn't really tried *that* hard. It was like knowing you were going to have a hangover in the morning but making the measured decision that it was worth it. *Good God,* she thought. *Let him be worth it…*

He pushed his chair back, and stood, stretching his long legs. Her heart squeezed at the sight of him in his Wranglers—every inch the tall, lean cowboy.

"What do you say?" he asked her. "Want to get some air? Might be good to walk off some pie, anyway."

"I'd like that."

"You two don't rush back," Daisy said. "Have fun."

He pulled the chair out for her, and she stood. He put his hand on the small of her back as they headed for the door and their jackets. She loved how it felt there, warm and subtly possessive. She never thought she'd be a woman who'd want to be possessed by anyone, but then again, she'd never met a man like Porter before, either. He was beginning to turn all the things she thought she knew about herself, inside out. Like whether or not she'd ever be a mother. Through his eyes, she saw herself as more than capable, more than worthy of that gift in her life. He was also making her question things that she thought she'd put to rest a long time ago. Like leaving the country. Like starting a new adventure somewhere other than Marietta, her new home that she was only now beginning to fall in love with.

She shrugged into her puffy blue jacket and zipped it up, feeling a torrent of these new emotions swirl in her heart. But the biggest emotion, the most significant one, had to do with Porter himself. She was falling for him, despite knowing better, despite trying to talk herself out of it. And that would change everything.

He opened the door for her, and she stepped out into the cold night air. It smelled like pine trees and animals, and she breathed deeply, a frosty cloud puffing from her lips.

They made their way down the porch steps and began walking side by side down the long drive. Their feet crunched in the gravel, and somewhere in the distance, an owl hooted softly. The cattle stood in the pastures on either side of them, nothing but quiet shadows in the silver pools of moonlight. Daisy was right—tonight was absolutely breathtaking.

"I'm glad you came," Porter said, breaking the silence.

"Thank you for inviting us."

"You make a mean apple pie. Has anyone ever told you

that?"

She laughed. "No, but I try. It was my mother's recipe. She loved to bake."

"I'm sorry, you know."

"About?"

"Your mom."

Justine had only recently told him about the loss of her mother. Described the last few years without her. Even though she'd been gone a while now, the pain still felt fresh sometimes. A lot of that had to do with reconciling with her dad. Her mom had still blamed him for leaving when she'd died, and she'd never forgiven him. It had been up to Justine and Jemma to forgive for her, and that had been a long, difficult journey.

She tucked her chin into the collar of her jacket, her breath warming her face. "Thank you," she said. "It still feels strange that she's not here."

"But you had her in your life. She died too soon, but at least you've got the memories. That's something."

THE WORDS WERE heavy with meaning, laced with pain. She knew he didn't have many memories of his mother, because she'd left. Justine's dad had left, too, but they'd been able to make new memories. Porter was in limbo, stuck somewhere between not having something, and being able to have it if he took the next step. It must be a strange feeling.

"You're right," she said. "The memories are a comfort."

They continued walking, their footsteps falling into a gentle rhythm.

"You know…I found my mom."

She stopped and turned to him. He stopped, too.

"You did?"

"Yeah. It actually wasn't that hard. Took a day or so, but the magic of the internet and all that."

His expression was stoic in the moonlight, unreadable. But she knew how confused he must be right then. She'd experienced it herself. Opening yourself up to the possibility of rejection from someone you loved felt like stepping up to a dark abyss, and wondering if you'd survive the fall.

Moving closer, she reached for his hand. His skin was rough—warm, despite the chill of the night. It had been a long, long time since she'd felt a connection like this with anyone.

"Have you contacted her yet?" she asked.

"I sent an email. Short and sweet."

"Has she answered?"

"Actually…she did. I'm not sure how to feel about any of this yet. But it's a start. If Cat can do it, so can I."

She squeezed his fingers. "What did she say?"

"Not much. She lives pretty close, though. Idaho. I guess I thought she'd be farther away than that."

Justine knew he was at a crossroads then. He just had to

decide which direction to take.

"I asked her if we could meet," he went on quietly. "Told her that we should talk in person. And she agreed…"

And there it is.

"I'm proud of you, Porter. This is a really big deal."

"Not sure my brothers would agree. They've made it pretty clear they don't need to see her again."

"And what about you?"

"I don't *need* to see her. I *want* to see her. There's a difference. For me, the end result isn't as important as going through the steps to try and make it happen. Does that make sense?"

"Perfect sense."

He smiled down at her. "You know, I've never talked about this with anyone before. Not really. And now, here I am, spilling my guts to you."

She smiled back. "How does that feel?"

"Weird. And good. Confusing, but I'm going with it."

"Weird and good is the story of my life."

He wrapped an arm around her waist and pulled her close.

"I'm not sure I want you to move all the way across the Atlantic next summer," he said, "and honestly, I don't know what to do with that."

It was what had been weighing on her the most lately. Having to leave Cat, having to leave Porter and the ranch. Leaving Jemma and her dad, so soon after moving to Marietta to be closer to them. It was all beginning to feel more and more like a mistake instead of the change she thought she'd wanted so badly. And she didn't know what to do with it either.

"We can write," she said, sounding unconvincing even to herself. "And FaceTime?"

"I can't kiss you over FaceTime."

He pushed his hand up the back of her sweater and pressed it against her bare skin. She shivered.

"I wasn't prepared for any of this, you know," he said. "I was doing just fine before you came along."

She knew what he meant. She'd been doing just fine, too. At least that's what she'd been telling herself.

"And now here we are," he continued. "With me making you feel guilty about leaving, and I don't do guilt. Ever."

"There's still time to put the brakes on, Porter. If this doesn't make sense, we just stop, right? And nobody gets hurt."

He nodded, his lips tilting slightly. "That's very sensible, Justine."

That was her. Sensible, boring, unwilling to stick her neck out for any kind of emotional connection. She'd thought going to Europe was taking a risk, but it was actually turning out to be just the opposite. A chance to run away. Again.

Moving his hand around to her rib cage, he dipped his head to kiss her neck. His scruff was scratchy against her skin, deliciously male. She tilted her head and closed her eyes for a second, reveling in his warmth, the way he made her feel. Like she was waking up after being asleep for years.

And then, he took her face in his hands, forcing her to look into his eyes. It was at that moment that she knew she wasn't just falling anymore. She was in love. Whatever had been set in motion a few weeks ago, had taken her heart with it. She no longer had control over whether or not she got hurt, or whether or not to put the brakes on. This was controlling her, not the other way around.

"The thing is," he said huskily, "that I don't really have any interest in being sensible right now. Do you?"

Staring up at him, she shook her head.

"Good. Then we agree on something."

Before she could respond, he leaned down the rest of the way and kissed her.

Lord help me, she thought.

And then she lost the ability to think altogether.

Chapter Twelve

"I CAN'T BELIEVE you're actually doing this," Griffin said, standing by the closet with his arms crossed over his chest. He was looking especially accountant-like today, his green collared shirt buttoned all the way up, and his khakis so starched, they'd probably stand up on their own.

Porter reached past him to grab a T-shirt, doing his best to ignore the look on his little brother's face. The one that said he was crazy. The one that said he was going to regret this. Which, yeah. He might. But at least he was taking a chance, which was more than he could say for the rest of his family.

"Why would you want to have anything to do with her, Porter? After the way she left us?"

Porter shoved the T-shirt into his duffel bag on top of his socks and toothbrush. He was only going to be gone overnight, so he wasn't taking much. Back tomorrow before the cattle needed fed.

"It's complicated," he said.

"Complicated isn't a strong enough word for it. Nuts is better."

Frowning, Griffin pushed his glasses up with his index finger. Dating Rae had loosened him up a lot. He'd even gotten a dog, which was huge. But he was still the most tightly wound of the Cole men, something that was on stark display at the moment. Griffin couldn't wrap his head around the fact that anyone would want to open themselves up to this. And Porter didn't blame him for that. He didn't need his understanding, necessarily. Just his support.

"Say what you really feel, little brother."

Griffin ignored that. "You've talked to Brooks?"

"Yep."

"And?"

"He's in the nuts camp with you."

"And Dad?"

"On board, I guess."

Griffin shoved a hand through his dark hair, making it stand straight up.

"You're awfully worked up about this, Griff," Porter said. "I didn't ask you to come with me, you know."

"Because you know I'd tell you to go to hell."

"Well, that's why I didn't ask."

He watched Griffin walk over to the window and look out at the ranch. The sun was bright in the cobalt-blue sky, but it was supposed to rain later. The first of several storm fronts that were supposed to move across Montana in the next week or so. Thanksgiving was getting closer, and so was the livestock auction. It was all giving Porter a weird sense of urgency that wasn't necessarily like him.

He wished this wasn't such a point of contention for his brother. He didn't want to piss him off or make him feel unsettled in any way. But at the same time, he knew it was something he had to do. In order to move on from the wounds of his childhood that had been dictating the way he'd been living his life up to now. And before he could help it, he thought of Justine. How would taking this step affect his relationships moving forward? He had no idea, of course, until he took it.

"Don't be mad, brother," he said. "You can't stay mad at me, right?"

Griffin turned to him, his jaw working. "I'm not mad…"

"Then what?"

"Worried, I guess. We were screwed up for a long time because of her."

"But we're not kids anymore."

"Yeah, I know that. But things are finally good here. Dad's doing great. He's settling into Marietta. People are getting to know him. We're all doing really well, considering. I just don't want to rock the boat. I don't know why *you'd* want to."

"Look…" Porter rubbed the back of his neck. "I don't know how to explain it, because I really don't understand myself. I feel the same way about Mom. She left us. It was unconscionable what she did. And I don't know if I can ever forgive that. But I'm at a point in my life where I need to be at peace with it. I thought I was before, but I wasn't. I can't trust anyone. Don't you think there's something wrong with that?"

"You're preaching to the choir, man."

"I know. I know it's been hard on you, too. But you've gotten past it enough to have some meaningful relationships in your life. You and Brooks...even Dad. I'm the only one who's still fighting it, and quite frankly, that's messed up."

That was a mild way of putting it, but it was the closest Porter could come to articulating how he felt. Messed up. Damaged. Weird. All of it fit.

Gritting his teeth, he tucked his shaving kit inside the duffel bag. The truth was, maybe Griffin would never understand this. But it didn't matter. It needed to be done anyway.

"Whatever happens," Griffin finally said, "I've got your back. Okay?"

Porter looked up at him. Sometime in the last few minutes, his chest had grown unbearably tight. Now, it felt like someone was squeezing him from behind. Squeezing the breath right out of him.

He'd never been a very emotional guy, which made this whole thing even more strange. But he guessed pain had to catch up to everyone eventually. Eventually, everyone had to reconcile with their past. He liked to think that finding his mother wasn't so much stupid, as it was brave. At least, that's what Cat had taught him.

"Thanks, brother," he said.

And found he didn't have the words for anything else.

JUSTINE PULLED UP to Diamond in the Rough with her heart in her throat. She hadn't planned on this; it had just happened. When Porter had texted her that morning, saying he was meeting his mother for dinner in Boise, she'd gotten a substitute, and asked Brooks and Daisy if Cat could spend the night with them at the ranch. She had no idea if offering to come with Porter would be welcome or not. But either way, she was here, so it was too late to back out now.

Taking a deep breath, she put her car in park and turned off the engine. She looked up just as Porter was walking down the porch steps. He smiled and waved, looking surprised to see her.

She opened the door and stepped out into the bright October morning.

"What's up?" he asked, coming around the front of her car. "Everything okay?"

"Everything's fine. I'm sorry, I should've called. I just knew you were leaving any time, and I had a few things to take care of at school…"

He glanced at his watch. "Did you get out early? Where's Cat?"

"He's still in class. I got a substitute."

Leaning down, he kissed her forehead. He smelled good, like leather and soap. He wasn't wearing his Stetson this morning, a rarity. His dark hair shone in the sunlight, making her want to touch it.

She took an even breath. "I know this is forward, so just tell me if you'd rather be alone, because I'd *completely* understand. But I thought you might want some support today. You won't even know I'm there."

He gazed down at her, a slow smile spreading across his lips. Two deep dimples cut into both cheeks. She probably shouldn't be so moved by those dimples at this point, but she absolutely was.

"Well, now," he said. "Not knowing you were there wouldn't be any fun."

The words were innocent enough, but there was insinuation. In his voice, in his tone. Because of course there would be the issue of where they would sleep tonight…

Her cheeks flooded with heat. It was hard not to be undone by the way he was looking at her. Like she'd just opened Pandora's box, which, she guessed she had.

"Don't worry," he said. "I'll be a complete gentleman, I promise."

That was the problem. She didn't know if she wanted to him to be a gentleman at all.

Chapter Thirteen

PORTER SAT IN the driver's seat of his truck, the engine running to keep the cab warm. Justine sat next to him; her face illuminated by the lights on the dash.

They'd stopped talking a few minutes ago and were lost in their own thoughts. Porter was still having a hard time believing that tonight, he'd be sitting across from his mother for the first time in twenty years. Able to ask the questions that had plagued him since boyhood. Able to finally tell her what lay in his heart.

He ground his teeth together. Before, when he'd told Griffin why he was doing this, it had seemed clearer. He'd felt more resolute. Here, now, with the heater blowing against his face, and Justine sitting beside him, he wasn't so sure.

Since finding his mom a week ago, they'd emailed back and forth. Just surface things, like what they did for a living, what kind of places they'd been on vacation. Things you might talk about with someone that you were waiting at a bus stop with. He hadn't gone deeper, figuring they'd get there soon enough anyway. But now he had to wonder from the tone of those emails, if she was planning on digging into the stuff that really mattered. Why she'd left. And if she'd missed her boys at all over the years.

Justine reached out and put her hand on his thigh. He hadn't thought about asking her to come. He just assumed he'd be doing this by himself, since asking for help had never been his strong suit. But having her along had filled him with a quiet sense of strength that he wasn't sure he'd be able to articulate if he tried.

Instead, he wrapped his fingers around hers and looked over. She smiled, her eyes full of warmth.

"How are you doing?" she asked.

He glanced at the clock on the dash. Almost time. His mom had told him what she'd be wearing—a white wool coat and tan slacks. But he knew he'd recognize her anyway. Her face was burned into his memory. Into his heart.

"I'm okay," he said. "A little nervous, I guess. But okay."

"Are you sure you want me to come? I can stay in the truck if that's easier."

"No, I want you there."

He leaned over and kissed her softly, desire stirring in his chest.

"Ready?" he asked, leaning away again.

"Ready."

They climbed out of the truck into the gritty fall evening. It was foggy, the mist settling around the Italian restaurant, making it look more like an apparition than a place to eat.

Inside, they were shown to a table by the window that looked out over the murky shops across the street.

Porter settled into his seat and looked at his watch again. Five thirty on the dot. He glanced around the restaurant, making sure they hadn't missed her walking in.

Justine shrugged her jacket off and draped it over the back of her chair. She was wearing a pale pink cardigan with little pearl buttons on the front. Her dark hair hung in loose ringlets past her collarbone, and her skin looked soft and translucent in the flickering candlelight.

"May I get you two something to drink?" the waiter asked.

"I'll have a glass of white wine, please," Justine said.

"And I'll have a beer. Whatever you have on tap. We might need a little time before we order. We're expecting someone else."

"Certainly."

The waiter disappeared, leaving them alone again.

Justine reached out and took his hand. "Just think," she said. "In a few weeks, Cat will be doing this."

Porter smiled, but it felt tight. He'd been thinking the exact same thing. And wondering more and more how smart that was. He was a grown man, and this meeting was making him feel like he was going to be sick all over his boots. He could only guess how an eleven-year-old would handle it.

Justine looked around. "She said five thirty?"

"Yup."

They were quiet as she tucked her hands back in her lap. They both knew tonight was a roll of the dice.

The waiter came back with their drinks, and Porter picked his beer up gratefully, taking a long gulp before setting it down again.

The front door opened and they looked over, but it was a little old man in an overcoat and a fedora.

Porter sat back in his chair. He felt like he wanted to crawl right out of his skin.

"She never called herself mom," he finally said, his voice low.

"What?"

He rubbed his thumb over the condensation on his mug and studied the trail of clarity it made on the glass.

"She never said mom. In her emails. When she signed off, she said Christina." He looked up. "Don't you think that's strange?"

Justine thought about this, her mouth curving into a frown.

"Maybe she was trying to be respectful," she said. "Maybe she thought she'd lost that right."

"Maybe. But it felt more significant than that." He looked at his watch again. She was twenty minutes late. But in reality, she was more like two decades late.

Justine watched him, her eyes sad. "What do you want to do?"

"I want to sit here with you and have a nice dinner. I want to drink my beer, and talk, and not think about how Griffin was probably right. How this was probably a big mistake."

"She might just be running late. Maybe it's the weather, or she had car problems…"

Porter felt his shoulders stiffen at the excuses. He didn't want to give his mother any more excuses. He was done with those.

"She's not running late," he said. "She's not coming."

And even though it was plausible that she might still walk through the door, he knew then that she wouldn't. He wasn't sure how that made him feel. Foolish? Hurt? Furious? Maybe all of the above. But mostly, he just felt tired.

Justine worried her bottom lip with her teeth. It was obvious she wanted to say something, but there was nothing left to say. He'd known what kind of woman his mother was, and just because several years had passed, he hadn't expected that she'd changed fundamentally. This stung, but it wasn't a surprise.

"Hey," he said. "It's okay. Really."

She didn't look convinced. In fact, her eyes were a little too bright, her face a little too flushed.

A distinctive heat crept up his neck, and he recognized it immediately as anger. So, that was the emotion that was going to push its way to the front of the line. He didn't fight it. Just sat there, letting it wash over him. Anger at his mother. Anger at her selfishness. Anger at himself for having any kind of hope that she might want to see him again. It wasn't okay. None of it was okay. And that was just something he was going to have to learn to live with. To get past, once and for all. But without any answers from his mother. Without any reckoning from her.

The waiter stopped at their table again, looking hesitant. Probably sensing the tension in the air.

"Do you folks need a little more time?"

Porter gazed over at Justine. *Time.* If he had all the time in the world, would he ever have anything to offer a woman like her? Would he ever be whole enough to try?

She smiled from across the table. "Yes, please," she said.

JUSTINE WATCHED PORTER step up to the window and pull the curtain back. The view was supposed to be overlooking downtown Boise, but the fog made it nearly impossible to see across the street. It cloaked the city in its eerie gray, the mist creeping past the hotel window like something alive. She shivered, even though they'd turned up the heat a few minutes ago.

Porter stood there staring outside as if he didn't see any of it. He'd been quiet since they'd left the restaurant, only answering her in short, clipped sentences. He was lost in thought, that was obvious. But she didn't know what to say to bring him back to her.

She got up from the bed and walked over, her footsteps quiet on the plush carpet. She knew he was wrestling with this. It didn't matter if you were fourteen or forty, she thought. The loss of a parent still hurt the same.

"Porter..."

He balled the curtain in his fist, and then let it go slowly, deliberately. It fell back into place, cutting the room off from the light outside the window.

"Yeah." He didn't turn around.

"You can talk to me," she said. She stepped up behind him but didn't touch him like she wanted to. She knew he would have to be the one to invite her into his thoughts tonight. Into his heart.

"I'm sorry," he said.

"For what?"

"For you coming all the way here. I thought it would be more of a satisfying trip. I sure as hell thought I might be in a better place with all of this."

She stared at the back of his head. She longed to reach up and run her fingertips down the nape of his neck. To trace his wide, muscular shoulders over his denim shirt. To turn him around and take his handsome face in her hands.

But she didn't. Yes, he needed to be the one to reach for her, for a lot of reasons. But she also knew that she couldn't reach for him because of her own fear. What if she let herself fall the rest of the way, and he didn't feel the same? What if he left her before she could leave him? All questions that were mired in old heartache and bitterness. She just couldn't stop thinking about her mother, and how she'd been absolutely broken after her dad left. Justine didn't want that to happen to her. As many feelings as she had for Porter, she was also fighting them every step of the way. Out of pure self-preservation.

As if reading her mind, he finally turned around. His face was bathed in shadow, the scruff on his jaw making him look dark and moody. His gaze found hers and pinned her in place.

"Why *are* you here?" he asked quietly.

Her heart was beating so hard, she could feel it thumping in her ears. Pounding out a rhythm that was like the ticking of a clock. Why was she here? It was an honest question, and one that she shouldn't have trouble answering, yet she did. Why was it so hard to tell someone how you felt about them? Why was it so hard to learn how to trust again? She needed to get to that place. She needed to find herself in all of this. To find her strength.

Licking her lips, she looked down at her hands. They were shaking. Her mother had never found her own strength.

When she looked up at Porter again, her stomach was curled into a tight little ball.

"Why did I come here…" she said.

He nodded, watching her, then reached out to tuck a

stray curl behind her ear. So tenderly, so sweetly. She'd found herself wondering over the years if men were even capable of such things. Or if they just faked it to get what they wanted. She wondered if the sweetness they offered would always be conditional or would have an expiration date. There certainly was for her poor mother.

But something about Porter Cole had opened her eyes to another kind of possibility. Another kind of man altogether. One who didn't inflict pain, at least not on purpose. And one who might not leave. At least not right away.

The realization made her take a step closer.

"I came here because I'm falling in love with you, Porter," she said, her voice catching. "That's why."

He stared down at her. In the hallway, someone walked by, jingling their keys. It was a stark reminder that the world beyond the two of them was still spinning, still functioning in its ordinary ways. Despite how Porter would respond to what she'd just said, the sun would still come up tomorrow in the east and go down in the west.

"You love me…" he said, letting his voice trail off.

She nodded. She didn't trust herself to say anything more. Besides, she didn't really *need* to say anything more. Loving him just about summed it up.

He swallowed visibly, his Adam's apple bobbing up and down, then put his hands in his pockets. "I guess this is the part where I remind you that neither one of us is looking for a relationship right now. And that you're leaving in a few months anyway."

"You could remind me of that," she said, forcing her chin up. "But I already know."

"And that we both have some fairly significant hang-ups."

"That's true."

"And you're still falling in love with me."

"Basically."

The expression on his face was unreadable. She was shaking so hard now, she was sure he'd be able to see from where he stood. Telling him how she felt had taken a certain amount of faith that she wasn't sure she'd be able to conjure up again. But no matter what happened, she was glad she'd said it. She *had* to learn how to take a chance, how to love again, or she'd end up locked behind her own stupid walls forever.

He rubbed the stubble on his chin, and then sighed, turning away from her. He stared out the window, and she was struck again by how handsome he was. How dark and brooding he could be.

"Well, I could say the same, Justine. I could tell you that I was falling in love with you, too. But it also wouldn't be fair to either one of us."

She had to remind herself to breathe. Had to swallow the aching lump in her throat. "What do you mean?"

"I mean, you're leaving." He turned to look down at her again. "Next summer you'll be gone. And I don't want you to have any guilt about that. You decided to move overseas for a reason. It's a big deal for you. It'd be a big deal for anyone. But I have to be honest here, too…"

She balled her hands into fists, trying to concentrate on the sting of her nails biting into her palms, over the throbbing in her heart. "Okay…"

"I'm not up for this," he said quietly. "I thought I was. I thought I was okay with being casual with you. But tonight…all of this. It's reminded of me who I really am. I've been alone all this time for a reason."

She willed her chin not to tremble, but it did anyway.

"Nothing good would come of it, Justine," he said. "Only pain."

Nodding, she took a step back. She was surprised her legs were holding her up at all. What had she expected, anyway? That he'd end up proposing? She knew what she was getting herself into the second she'd kissed him. He'd never lied to her.

"I thought I was prepared for my mom not showing up tonight," he continued, his voice hoarse. "I mean, the woman has been a no-show my entire life. But I opened myself up for this…this *disappointment*, even though I knew better. I *knew* how it would feel if she pulled this shit. I've been telling myself that taking a chance on her would help me move on, and there's some truth to that. But the entire truth, is that I wanted to take a chance on her. I wanted it to work out."

He blinked down at her, and for one horrible second, she didn't think she could stand the look in his eyes. The pain there, the heartache. Not when she was fending off her own heartache. They really were a match made in hell.

"Do you see what I'm saying?" he continued. "Am I making any sense?"

She nodded again. Perfect sense. Painful, awful, perfect sense.

"You leaving in a few months wouldn't just disappoint me," he said. "It would break my damn heart. I know that, it's a fact. Just like I knew what might happen with my mom. The only difference is, you and I can stop this now, and save ourselves a lot of grief in the long run."

He was right. Of course he was. It wasn't what she wanted to hear, but it was the most sensible thing. *Would* she be prepared to cancel her move to Europe for an affair that would only be a few months old when it was time to leave? This teaching job was something she'd dreamed of for years. A once-in-a-lifetime opportunity. And before she could help it, she wondered if Porter Cole was also a once-in-a-lifetime opportunity.

She touched her temple at a sudden pounding there.

He frowned. "Say something."

"I understand. I do. There needs to be a balance in life, right? Taking risks, with being realistic.... We'd be a big risk."

He pulled in a breath like he was about to answer. But

didn't. For a second, she wondered if he was telling her how he honestly felt. But then she pushed the question away where it couldn't spark and start some kind of fire inside of her.

No, better to follow his lead on this. It didn't mean she'd never be brave with her heart again. It just meant that right now, at this precise moment in time, it wasn't the smartest thing to do.

"I wouldn't ever want to be a mistake for you," he said quietly. "You deserve more."

She didn't know about deserving more, but she wanted more, that was for sure. But people didn't always get what they wanted. That was life. Right now, that was her life.

"You'd never be a mistake, Porter," she said. "No matter what."

He pulled her into his arms. It felt different now. Like he was holding a part of himself back, which, she guessed he was. But he was warm and solid, and she lay her head against his chest, grateful for what he was offering.

Without saying anything else, he kissed the top of her head. She closed her eyes, taking it in. Taking it all in, before they did the sensible thing and moved onto friendship where there wouldn't be any more kisses on the lips.

And even though they were doing this to avoid broken hearts, Justine's broke just the same.

Chapter Fourteen

PORTER LEANED AGAINST the round pen, watching Cat brush the leggy black colt. Wookiee was turning out to be a precocious little thing, which matched Cat's personality to a tee. He kept trying to grab Cat's jacket in his teeth, a game he'd learned from his mama.

Cat sidestepped expertly. This was good for both of them. Cat was learning how to handle baby animals, and Wookiee was learning how to be handled. Win, win.

Grabbing the foal by his halter, Cat ran the brush down his back. "I think he likes it."

"I *know* he likes it. Keep doing what you're doing. He'll learn how to be a horse from Abby, but he'll figure out his relationship with humans from us. It's really important that he get a lot of positive interactions from the beginning."

It was a cold day—blustery, making the freckles stand out on Cat's ruddy cheeks. He'd gained a little weight over the last few weeks, that was obvious. He and Justine had made a habit out of coming out to the ranch for dinners, and Daisy decided early on that Cat would be her pet project. She loved to cook, but even more than that, she loved watching people enjoy her cooking. Especially growing boys who might need a few extra calories here and there.

At the thought of dinners with Justine, Porter's stomach dropped. Ever since Boise, she'd been distant. He couldn't blame her for that. After all, this was his way. Whenever things got serious, he'd shove people out of his life, so they wouldn't affect it any more than necessary. And up until now, it had worked just fine. He'd been perfectly happy with shallow relationships and one-night stands.

But something about this time was different. And he knew why. He was in love. Without sleeping with her, without even getting to second base. It was ironic, and very unlike him. But here he was.

Frowning, he looked up to see Cat watching him.

"What's wrong, Porter?" he asked.

"Nothing, Champ. Nothing's wrong."

"That's not true. I can tell."

Porter knew that Justine had told him about the fiasco with his mother. He didn't know if she'd told him about the email his mom had sent the next morning, apologizing. Telling him she wasn't ready yet. That she loved him, but maybe she'd never be ready. She was ashamed of herself, but apparently not too ashamed to make it right.

"It's just been a hard couple of days," he said. "Nothing to worry about."

Cat put the brush down and walked over to lean against the fence. Wookiee followed him like a puppy, then got distracted by Clifford, who was rolling in something a few feet away.

"I know what happened with your mom," Cat said quietly.

Porter looked over at him. Such a sweet, sensitive kid. But tough as the day was long.

"Oh yeah?"

"Justine told me."

"I thought she might."

"Are you sad?"

"No. Maybe a little disappointed. Maybe a little mad at myself. But not sad, really."

"Because it's okay to be sad, you know."

Porter nodded. Maybe he was sad. He'd spent so much time denying that particular emotion, he didn't even know anymore.

"And you're probably worried about taking me to the livestock auction," Cat continued. "We could see my dad and he could do the same thing to me."

"That's true. I'm not going to lie."

"It's okay. I think about it, too."

"Yeah?"

Cat shrugged. "But I'm not going to let it stop me. And it's good that it didn't stop you, either. Because now you know how your mom is. She doesn't deserve to get to know you again, right? She doesn't deserve to get to know Brooks and Griffin, either. And now you don't have to wonder about her anymore."

Porter felt his lips stretch into a smile. *Out of the mouths of babes.*

"How'd you get to be so smart?"

Cat grinned. Gap toothed, freckled faced. Looking happy as he turned his attention back to Wookiee.

Porter was quiet for a few minutes, watching the boy and horse enjoy each other's company. The sun had come out and was warm on the back of his neck. He thought of Justine, wondering what she was doing right then. If she might be thinking of him.

He cleared his throat. "Hey, Champ…"

"Yeah."

"How's Justine doing? When she dropped you off, she didn't stick around long."

"She's okay. Busy with grading and junk. Getting ready for Thanksgiving break."

"Ahh."

"Why? Do you miss her?" There was a sparkle in Cat's eyes.

"Sure," he said. "Sure, I miss her. But she's got a lot going on."

"Well, she misses you, too."

His heart stumbled at that. Betraying him. Making him feel like he didn't have any control here, no matter how hard he wanted it. But that's what love did. It made a fool of you every time. He wasn't in control. And neither was Justine.

He pulled his Stetson low over his eyes, not anxious for Cat to read his expression right then.

"You should call her," Cat said matter-of-factly.

"Oh...well..."

"I know you two like each other."

"Sure, we like each other."

"Not like that. Not like friends."

Porter shook his head. "It's not that easy."

"Why not?"

"For one thing, she's got a job that's taking her out of the country pretty soon." He knew that Cat was more than aware of this fact, since it also meant he'd be going back to Missoula. Porter wondered if Nola would be well enough to take care of him by then. How he'd do back there. If he'd start fighting again, if he'd slip back to that dark place where he'd been before. All questions that would be answered soon enough.

"And for another," he continued, "I've got my hands full with this place. It doesn't leave a ton of time for a new relationship." It was more than he'd been planning on sharing, but Cat seemed to take it in stride.

"It's the slow season," Cat said. "Remember? You said it yourself. Pretty soon there won't be many guests."

"Yeah, I did say that. But that doesn't mean there aren't guests now." He looked at his watch, remembering he was supposed to be giving a lasso lesson at eleven. He was better at these kinds of lessons than Brooks, who was admittedly shit at hitting any kind of moving target.

"And so what if she takes that new job?" Cat said. "That doesn't mean you can't like someone just because they're leaving. I like her, and I know she's leaving."

Porter stared at him. What could he possibly say to that, since it was absolutely true?

"I know, Champ," he said. "But it's more complicated than that."

"Why? What's complicated about it? If you like someone, like them."

"I could say the same about you and Amber."

"How's that the same?"

"You like her, right?"

Cat considered this. Then sighed. "Yeah."

"And she likes you." He held a hand up before Cat could deny it. "It's pretty obvious."

"What*ever*."

"But just because you like each other, doesn't mean it's as easy as all that. You haven't called her yet, have you?"

Cat raised his small chin, suddenly looking like a force to be reckoned with. "No. But I will if you will."

"You mean call Justine?"

"Sure."

"I don't…"

"I know. You were going to punk out. But that's what I'm here for, remember?"

Porter sighed. "Okay. Alright, I'll give her a call. Will

that make you happy?"

"Yes," Cat said simply. He seemed satisfied.

"But it doesn't mean anything, okay? It just means that I'm saying hi. That's it."

"I know."

"And you're going to call Amber?"

"Yeah. But I don't know what to say."

"Why don't you ask her to the movies or something?"

Cat narrowed his eyes. "You think she'd want to?"

"I do. But even if she says no, that's the worst that can happen, right?"

"I guess," Cat said, snapping Wookiee's lead rope back on. "I guess you're right. So, if that's true, if you asked Justine to stay in Marietta, the worst she could say is no."

Porter laughed. "I think you might be missing your calling as an attorney."

Cat looked pleased with himself.

"Why don't you take that little guy back out to the pasture with his mom," Porter said, pushing off the fence. "I've gotta get over to the barn for that lesson."

"Can I come?"

"Sure thing. How's your throwing arm?"

"It's pretty awesome."

Smiling at that, Porter headed toward the barn. Cat had started out with chores at the ranch in exchange for lessons, but now he was basically here every day. Absorbing everything, soaking it in like a sponge. It was painfully clear how much he'd come into his own here. And he'd have to leave it all behind next summer.

Porter felt the smile fade on his lips. The reality was, he wouldn't just be losing Justine in a few months, he'd be losing Cat, too. The weight of that settled squarely on his shoulders for the very first time.

And all of a sudden, he felt like putting his head in his hands.

Damn.

Chapter Fifteen

JUSTINE SAT WITH her head bent over her grade book, her curls brushing the top of her trusty red pencil. Henry, the janitor, was mopping the hallway outside her room, and humming some nameless tune. Every now and then, he'd jingle his keys, and remind her that she really needed to get a life.

It was Friday night, and Cat had wanted to stay the night at the ranch—something about the vet coming out to see Alloy. So she'd decided to stay late and work on grades. Staying late had never fazed her in the past. She loved her job, and especially enjoyed the solitude of a quiet, near-empty school where she could catch up on work. But tonight, it felt a little sad. She'd grown so used to having Cat around, that with him gone, her world felt a little less warm. A little less colorful.

And then there was Porter. She looked up with a sigh, letting her gaze fall on the poster of Abraham Lincoln across the room. He stared somberly back, his expression mirroring the somberness in her heart.

Honest Abe... He couldn't tell a lie. And most of the

time, Justine couldn't, either. But over the last few days she'd begun to wonder if she was being honest with herself. Her decision to move overseas had started out as a solid choice. A choice that she was excited about, that she was looking forward to. But lately, she'd been having to come up with reasons why it was still a good idea.

She put down her pencil and rubbed her eyes.

"Ms. Banks," Henry said, poking his bald head into her doorway. "There's someone here to see you."

She raised her brows. "Oh?"

"Says her name is Nola. She says she stopped by your place but you weren't home, and that she figured you'd be here burning the midnight oil."

Justine's heart jumped. She hadn't seen her friend in months, but Nola had told her she was going to surprise her one of these days. She just hadn't thought it would be so soon.

"Thanks, Henry!" she said. "You can just send her on back if you don't mind."

He nodded and disappeared again.

Justine began putting her paperwork away, excited as a little kid. She hadn't realized how much she'd missed her friend, how much she'd longed to see her in person, until just now. She knew Nola had lost her hair, and had also lost some weight, so Justine had been careful not to push a visit until she was ready. She felt like her coming tonight was a good sign. A sign that pointed to her getting better.

"Knock, knock!"

She looked up to see her friend in the doorway, beaming from ear to ear. She wore a purple jacket, and a lovely white scarf wrapped loosely around her head. Her cheeks were full of color, her hazel eyes sparkling. She looked absolutely beautiful.

"Oh my goodness!" Justine said, getting up and pulling her in for a hug. "I love your surprises!"

"*Ooomph.* You're gonna break me."

"Sorry!" Laughing, Justine pulled away, but kept both hands on her friend's shoulders to get a good look at her. "You look amazing. Just amazing. How do you feel?"

"I feel amazing, if you can believe that. Had my last treatment a few weeks ago, and the doc thinks I'm headed for a full recovery. I wanted to tell you in person." Nola pulled out a small plastic chair and sat down. "No guarantee, but I have a good feeling."

Justine sat across from her. "This is the best news. Just the best news ever."

"It's pretty great, right?"

"I'm so happy you're here. I've missed you."

"Oh, honey. I've missed you, too. I appreciate you keeping Cat away like you have. I didn't want him to see me feeling so poorly."

Justine grinned. "He's going to be so excited. He's out at the ranch tonight, but I'll go get him."

"No, no, don't do that. I'll see him in the morning. You

and I can gab like we used to. I wasn't sure what you had going on though, so I made a reservation at the Graff, just in case."

"Oh, no you don't." Justine patted her friend's knee. "You're staying with me."

"If you're sure… I'm not interrupting a hot date with your handsome cowboy?"

Justine sat back in her chair and it squeaked underneath her. She'd told Nola about Porter, but she'd left out the one major detail of falling in love with him. Now, with her sitting so close, with such a loving expression on her face, all she wanted to do was confide in her.

"No hot date," she said. "But here's the thing… I kind of let myself start caring about him."

Nola watched her. "How much caring are we talking about here?"

"You'd have to meet him, Nola. He's just this, this…force to be reckoned with."

"Justine."

She twisted the small gold ring on her pinkie finger. A Christmas gift from her dad. "Yes?"

"How much caring are we talking about?"

She pulled in a breath. Then let it out slowly. "I love him."

Nola sat back in her chair.

From down the hallway, they could hear Henry pushing the mop bucket along. Time seemed to be slowing down, with Justine's heart thumping steadily against her rib cage. She hadn't even told Jemma how she truly felt about Porter yet. She loved her little sister dearly, but sometime over the last few years, Nola had become Justine's touchstone. Her true north. The moment felt significant, and a small lump formed in the back of her throat.

"I love him," she said again. "But that's where it ends."

Nola held up a hand. Her nails were freshly painted, bubble gum pink. "Now, wait just a minute, pumpkin. Hold up."

"It wouldn't work."

"How do you know?"

She shook her head. "We talked about it the other night. I told him how I feel, and he reminded me that I'm leaving. Starting a brand-new relationship from overseas doesn't make any sense. I know that. And so does he."

"But—"

"And he's not ready anyway."

"Did he say that?"

"Basically. Basically he said it."

"Hmm…" Nola tapped her lips with her index finger.

"What?"

"I'm just absorbing this. Since you don't exactly fall in love easily, Justine. Not in all the time we've known each other. And that's not for a lack of me trying."

"That's true."

"So, maybe this whole thing isn't as cut and dry as you

say."

Justine frowned. "What do you mean?"

"I mean, maybe you need to take moving away out of the equation. Figure out how you feel about him without that complication in the mix."

"But it *is* in the mix."

"Will you just humor me for a second? Please?"

Justine exhaled softly. Nola was an expert at peeling layers away. She was the one who'd helped Justine finally forgive her father. She was the one who'd walked her through the complicated emotions surrounding her mother's death, and all the pain it had left behind. Other than Jemma, Nola knew her best in the whole world. So it wasn't a surprise that she'd be demanding a closer look at her love life now. She simply didn't want her to make a mistake. If the shoe were on the other foot, Justine would be doing the same.

"Okay," she said. "I'll humor you."

"Good. Good girl. So, you love him…"

"Yes."

"And he loves you? I mean, how could he not?"

"You're the only person who thinks I'm so lovable."

"That's not true. Cat loves you. And so does your sister, and so does your dad, and so do all your students. I think that's part of the problem here."

"What is?"

"I think you've spent so much time telling yourself that

you don't deserve love, that you've actually started believing it."

Justine gazed at her friend. Maybe she had a point. Maybe she didn't think she deserved love. Especially not Porter's. It was so like her to sabotage every chance at happiness she had. It was just easier to tell herself that something wouldn't work, that it wasn't right, than to dig deeper where the sharp things were.

She tapped a fingernail against the chair.

Nola watched her. "Are we getting somewhere?"

"You don't think I should take this job."

"I didn't say that."

"You *do* think I should take it."

"I didn't say that either."

"What do you think I should do?"

"Honey," Nola said, leaning forward. "I think you need to do what makes you happy, and let go of the rest. I'm here to tell you that life is short, and so precious that I don't have the words for it. Don't waste a single second of it being afraid."

Sudden tears prickled Justine's eyes. For her, tears had always been a sign of weakness. A lesson her mother had instilled at a young age. *Never let them see you cry!* But she was beginning to realize that feeling deeply wasn't a weakness. It could actually be a great strength. It was for Nola. It could be for her, too, if she'd trust herself enough with it.

"Now," Nola said gently. "You just have to figure out

what's going to make you happy, and go from there."

"I wish it were that easy."

"I know, pumpkin."

Sniffing, Justine reached for a Kleenex from her desk.

"Hey," Nola said. "Why don't you finish up here, and we can go grab a glass of wine somewhere. I think tonight calls for Chardonnay. You can tell me how Cat's doing. And then fill me in on this Porter fellow. I need a bigger picture."

"I'd love that," Justine said.

And meant every word.

JUSTINE SAT IN her darkened living room, looking out the window to the snow falling outside. The first real snow of the season. The world was peaceful and quiet, and her head was still pleasantly fuzzy from the wine with Nola. Her friend was asleep in the guest room, where Justine could hear her soft snores from down the hallway. Her house felt warm and cozy. But when she'd tried closing her eyes, she'd only been able to toss and turn.

She pulled her throw blanket up to her chin and watched the snowflakes falling underneath the streetlamp. Nobody had driven down her street in about twenty minutes, and the tire tracks were beginning to disappear. The drifts were getting thicker and fluffier, and she smiled, remembering the winter rituals she'd shared with Jemma as kids.

They'd had a dog when they were little. Greta. She loved the snow. She used to run around in circles snapping it up in her little jaws, making Jemma and Justine peel with laughter. Those had been good days. Simpler days. As a little girl, she never would have imagined that only a few years later, her father would leave, and her mother would change from a happy, carefree person, to someone whose anger and bitterness would eventually be passed on to her daughters.

Justine wrapped a curl absentmindedly around her finger. Things had ended badly for her family, but when it had been good, it had been really good. She missed those days. She missed walking to school with Jemma, her small hand tucked inside Justine's. She missed coming home to warm peanut butter cookies, and her mom's faded red apron tied snugly around her waist. She missed Greta, and how she'd sleep in Justine's lap when they watched TV. She missed all of it.

She sighed, wondering why she'd never gotten around to getting a dog when she'd moved out. She'd planned on it, but then one thing would lead to another, and it never seemed like the right time. She'd always wanted another dog, though. She chewed the inside of her cheek. *Technically*, she could have one now. She could go to the shelter tomorrow, if she wanted, and bring one home.

She imagined the look on Cat's face if she were to walk through the door with a dog. But then she remembered there was no way she could have a pet. Of course. *You're leaving, remember?*

At the thought, there was no denying the stab of pain in her heart. It made her so sad. But she had to figure out *why* it made her sad. Was it because she didn't want to leave Porter? Sure. That was a big part of it, of course. But what about leaving Cat? She and Nola had talked a lot tonight about how much Cat loved it here. How hard it would be for him to move back to Missoula. He missed Nola fiercely, but he was a ranching kid at heart, it was obvious now. And what were they going to do about that? Nola had said she would try and find a good place for him to take lessons near her place, but Justine could tell the thought of taking him away from Diamond in the Rough unsettled her. Justine could relate.

She shifted on the couch, feeling restless. The livestock auction was only a few days away now. Not only was Cat having to face leaving the ranch, but he was also facing the uncertainty of seeing his dad again. She couldn't help but picture the grief on Porter's face after his mother had stood him up. She'd wanted to wrap her arms around him, to fix it somehow. But it was something he'd had to bear. She could hardly stand the thought of the same thing happening to Cat.

A sudden lump formed in her throat. Somewhere along the line, she'd managed to let herself fall in love, get attached to a tween boy, and catch glimpses of a future inside a little town that she hadn't expected to adore so much. This wasn't how it was supposed to have gone. She was supposed to be planning her move, getting ready for her new job, her big adventure.

Instead, she found herself crying for the second time that night. She was so confused, she didn't know which way was up. But one thing was becoming more and more clear… If she decided to stay in Marietta, it had to be for the right reasons. Not because she was afraid of the pain that leaving would bring.

Nola was right—she had to figure out what was going to make her happy.

And then grab onto it with both hands.

Chapter Sixteen

PORTER STOOD IN line at The Melt, the little grilled cheese café that Griffin's girlfriend, Rae Woods, owned and operated. He'd come into town to grab a few things at Marietta Western Wear and had been hungry, so he'd swung by on the way back to the ranch. Some toasted cheese had sounded pretty damn good, and Rae was the queen of toasted cheese.

The snow was still coming down, had been since last night. The café was crowded, and he kept his hands in his pockets and his arms close to his body as people squeezed by to pick up their to-go orders. The entire place smelled like french fries and bread, and his stomach growled.

Behind him, the door opened with the tinkle of a bell, and a gust of cold air brushed the back of his neck.

"Next!"

The line moved up and he moved with it, lost in thought.

"Porter?"

He turned. Standing there looking like an angel in an ivory cardigan and matching beret, was Justine. She smiled wide, her shoulders dusted with snow.

"What are you doing here?" she asked. "I'm not used to seeing you in town."

He looked down at her, taking her in, wanting more than anything to lean down and kiss her. But she wasn't his girlfriend. She wasn't even someone he was pursuing anymore, because they'd decided against it. Someone had forgotten to tell his heart, which thumped painfully at the sight of her.

"Grilled cheeses," he said, his voice rough. "My favorite childhood meal. Did I ever tell you that?"

She shook her head.

"There was a time when it was all my brothers and I would eat," he continued. "Made traveling extra fun. My dad had to plan all our pitstops ahead to make sure there was a grilled cheese on the menu."

She laughed. "Well, it didn't affect you growing up nice and strong. Maybe more little boys need to be picky eaters."

"Wish you'd been around to tell my mother that. It drove her batshit crazy." At the thought of his mom, he looked down at his boots for a second. He was still grappling with where she fit into his life now, into his childhood memories. It was getting harder and harder to make room for her there.

Justine ran her tongue over her lips, and they glistened underneath the café lighting. His throat suddenly felt very dry. This woman had been in his arms just a few short weeks ago. He'd been kissing those lips by a warm fire and reveling in the feel of her body pressed against his. Now, they were making small talk. It didn't feel right. In fact, everything about it felt wrong.

She glanced out the frosty window. There were people making their way down the sidewalk in boots and mittens, some of them holding steaming drinks and shopping bags. Thanksgiving was right around the corner. Soon, the ranch would be decked out in her finest Christmas attire, sparkling lights and fresh evergreen wreaths in every window. He wondered what Justine's plans were for Thanksgiving. If maybe she and Cat, her dad and sister, would want to spend it at Diamond in the Rough with him and his family.

She smiled wistfully, as if seeing something far away, then looked back, her eyes bright. "Don't you love the snow? It's just magical."

He nodded. He knew exactly what she meant—most locals would. Winter in Marietta was special.

"Next!"

The line moved up, but he and Justine didn't move with it. Instead, they stepped out of the way at the same time. He wasn't in the mood to rush this, and it looked like she wasn't either.

"I've missed you," she said quietly.

"I've missed you, too. Next time you bring Cat out, you should stay for coffee."

"I'd love that. But that's how this whole thing started,

remember? I don't think we can be trusted with coffee."

"Truthfully, I don't think we can be trusted with seeing each other at a sandwich shop, either. If how I feel is any indication."

She laughed. "What are we going to do about that? Seems like a problem."

"Depends on how you look at it. I can think of plenty of things to fix it."

"Yeah?"

"Sadly, none of them involve clothes."

She flushed as a woman in line looked over at that.

"You're terrible," she whispered.

They were quiet for a minute, as the front door opened and a red-cheeked couple walked through, rubbing their hands together.

"So..." Justine said. "The livestock auction is this weekend."

He nodded. He'd been thinking about it nonstop. Running through all the scenarios in his head and trying to prepare for them.

"Cat's so excited," she continued. "Do you still think Calvin will be there?"

"I think it's a good possibility."

"You know, Nola and I talked about this during her visit."

He watched her. She'd brought Nola along when she'd picked up Cat the other day, and he'd gotten to meet her.

She was one of those people that you felt like you'd known forever. A very sweet, very special lady. And he'd been able to see Cat in her instantly. His spunk obviously ran in the family.

"How is she feeling about it?" he asked, hoping on some strange level, that maybe she'd changed her mind, and wouldn't want Cat to go. But knowing that probably wasn't the case. It made sense that Cat should be able to choose for himself. No matter how complicated the decision was.

"She's anxious. But she knows it's the right thing."

Porter nodded.

"But we also talked about his future," she continued. "With or without Calvin wanting to be a part of it."

"His future…"

"The fact that when I leave, he'll be going back to Missoula. And what that will look like for him."

And there it was. The familiar ache at the thought of Justine leaving. And now, at the thought of Cat leaving, too. He didn't know when the idea of having them in his life had implanted itself in his heart, but in his heart, it absolutely was. Whether he liked it or not. Now, he just had to figure out how to deal with that. How to get past it, without getting down on his knees and begging them to stay.

Justine looked down at her hands for a second, seeming to compose herself. When she looked back up, her eyes were unmistakably misty. "No matter what, he's going to have a lot of adjusting to do."

"Yes," Porter said. "But he's a tough kid. He'll be okay."

"Will he, though? How do you know for sure?"

He didn't. Nobody did. The truth was, it would be hard on Cat, like she said. But he'd get through it. The first of many of life's curveballs that would be thrown at him over the years.

Reaching out, he took her hand. Her skin was warm, soft, and he rubbed his thumb over the backs of her knuckles.

"Next!"

The line moved up again, but all of a sudden, he wasn't hungry anymore. All he could concentrate on was the woman standing in front of him. The feel of her hand in his. The tilt of her lips, the look in her eyes. What if he did ask her to stay? What would she say to that? He imagined her staring up at him, trying to think of a way to let him down easy. Thinking of a way not to break his heart, because she'd thought about it, and he'd been right. There was no way it would work.

"The most important thing," he said, his voice low, "is that you've given him this time in Marietta. He wouldn't have had that otherwise, and I think it's been good for him. I think it's helped him settle into a better place."

A lady in a pink knit hat squeezed by and apologized under her breath. Outside the window, the snow was coming down harder now. An early storm promising a white winter.

"You're right," she said. "Marietta has been wonderful

for him. You've been wonderful for him."

"I can't take the credit. Thank Abby and Wookiee."

"And Alloy and Clifford, and Brooks and Daisy…"

"Hey, it takes a village."

With a small squeeze, he let go of her hand. Her expression fell for a second. So briefly that he barely caught it.

"We'd better get back in line," she said. "Or we'll be here all afternoon."

He looked at his watch. "You know, I don't have to be back for another hour. And there's an empty table over there. Want to have lunch?"

It wasn't exactly asking her to cancel her trip. But it was the best he could do under the circumstances.

She smiled. "I'd love that."

Chapter Seventeen

THE MORNING OF Marietta's livestock auction dawned clear and cold. The naked maple trees outside Justine's kitchen window sparkled with frost, their thin limbs reaching for the bright blue sky.

She stood at her stove, scrambling some eggs for Cat, and dumping in some extra shredded cheese at the last minute. It was a big day. He was going to need all the fuel he could get.

For the tenth time that morning, she pictured him walking up behind Calvin and tapping him on the shoulder. She imagined the man turning to look down at his son. His son whom he hadn't seen, or even bothered to contact in years. And for the tenth time that morning, her stomach turned.

But then she'd remind herself that Cat might not even see him there. After all, it didn't seem like he really wanted to be found.

She looked up to see Cat shuffle into the room and pull out a chair at the table. It was early, barely seven, but he'd showered and put on jeans and a collared shirt. Western-style, blue denim. His red hair was combed neatly to the side, and his freckles stood out on his pale face. He looked scared to death.

"Good morning," she said, smiling a little too wide. "How'd you sleep?"

"Okay."

"I'm making you cheesy eggs, your favorite. With a strawberry Pop-Tart on the side."

"Thanks, Justine."

She moved the eggs around in the pan, and they sizzled comfortingly.

"So," she said. "I heard you talking on the phone last night. It was late. Did you call your grandma?"

"No. That was Amber."

She raised her brows but tried not to look too surprised. He'd only mentioned Amber to her the other day. Something about a bet with Porter. But then he'd seemed nervous about it, so she hadn't pushed, even though she was so curious, she could barely stand it. Other than the fight on the field trip, Cat had been quiet and reserved since coming to Marietta. It was only recently that he'd come out of his shell with his classmates. He'd hung out with a boy named Kota the other day. They'd gone out to the ranch for a trail ride. But he'd been slower to warm up to any girls, so this was a first.

"Oh yeah?" she said.

He shrugged, some color creeping into his cheeks. "She's really nice."

Justine sprinkled some salt and pepper over the eggs and

turned the heat down. "She does seem nice. I know her folks."

"Her grandma died a few months ago. She's still really sad about it."

He lowered his head and touched a worn spot on the tablecloth. Gently, like he was afraid to call attention to it.

Watching him, Justine's heart squeezed. Even though he didn't talk about it much, she knew he worried about Nola constantly. The visit last weekend had been good for him. He'd needed to see her in order to ease his mind a little.

She scooped the eggs onto a plate and carried them over with a glass of orange juice. "Here you go, honey. The Pop-Tart is toasting."

He smiled. "Thank you."

She sat down next to him and put her chin in her hand. She liked watching him eat. He'd definitely grown since he'd come to stay with her. He was filling out, filling in. Looking older for sure.

"So…" she began slowly. Not knowing quite how to word what she wanted to say next. *No matter what happens today, I'll be here for you…* The thought skittered across her mind, leaving a pulsing trail in its wake. She wanted him to know that he was loved. That she didn't want him to get hurt. That she was desperate to protect him and keep him happy inside his little bubble at the ranch. But of course, that wasn't realistic. None of them knew what would happen at the livestock auction today. Nobody knew how he'd settle in once he was back in Missoula. Or how she'd feel once she got to London. But she could guess well enough. At the moment, her heart felt like it might break in half.

He looked up at her. His normally bright eyes were deep and dark in the early light of the morning. "I know," he said. "You're worried about today."

"I just want to say that I care about you very much, Cat. You're a very special boy."

He looked down at his eggs and poked at them with his fork. So far, he hadn't taken a bite. Maybe he wouldn't be able to eat at all. "Thanks, Justine," he said.

"And I'm not the only one. Porter and Brooks and Daisy… They all think you're pretty amazing."

He nodded.

"Cat…"

He looked up at her again.

"If you see your dad today, if you don't see him today…I just want you to know that we're all proud of you. So, so proud."

He swallowed visibly. An expression crossed his face that she couldn't quite place, but it was obvious that he was trying to compose himself. And then he took a swig of orange juice, before setting the glass down and wiping his mouth with the back of his hand.

"I know it might not go great," he said, his gaze settling on hers. "And that will suck if it doesn't. But I want to at least try."

"I know…"

"And Justine?"

"Yes?"

"I care about you, too. I'm glad I got to stay with you for a while. I really like it here."

"I know you do, buddy."

"I didn't want to leave my grandma, but I know it was the right thing. She needed to get better without me there."

"Well, I know she misses you. She misses you a lot."

"Yeah. But she's pretty old, and it's hard for her to be raising a kid at her age."

Justine smiled at that. Nola was barely sixty, but to Cat, she might as well be pushing ninety-five.

"I'm glad you got to come stay, too," she said.

"I'm going to miss you when you go. And I'm gonna miss the ranch and Porter, and everyone. Especially Wookiee. He's awesome."

Cat leaned forward then and took a bite of eggs. She was glad.

"But we don't have to be talking like this," she continued quietly. "We don't have to worry about leaving for a while yet. We can just enjoy it while it lasts, right?"

"Yep."

She watched him carefully, trying not to look like she was watching him carefully. Right then, he reminded her of a delicate spring bud—struggling to break through the soil to the sunlight on the other side. He was trying so hard to be strong, trying to lean into what was happening to him, instead of fighting it, like he'd fought his entire life.

Pushing away from the table, she got up to get his Pop-Tart, so he wouldn't see the tears in her eyes.

PORTER DROVE SLOWLY through the muddy parking lot, trying not to splash the people walking by. The fairgrounds were packed full of trucks and trailers. Country music thumped from the covered arena to their right, and several food trucks were parked close, the smell of cooking meat wafting through the air.

It was a cold day, with a fine mist clinging to the windshield, but nobody seemed to mind. Most of the snow from the other day had melted away, so people had come out in droves. It felt like a big country party.

Beside him in the passenger's seat, Cat was quiet. He hadn't said much since leaving the ranch, only making small talk every now and then to break the silence. He'd told Porter about calling Amber and they'd joked a little about their bet, but mostly, he'd just stared out the window.

Porter glanced over at him now. He wore a camo baseball cap, and one of Brooks's old Carhartt jackets that was too big for him. He was every bit a rancher's kid. He was also a good kid with a big heart. And today, he might get it completely broken.

Working his jaw, Porter pulled into a parking space between two horse trailers and put the truck into park. He cut the engine and took a deep breath, wanting to say something to help Cat with this, but not knowing what. The truth was, he understood firsthand what was at stake here, and that last thing he wanted was to lie to him.

"How are you doing, Champ?" he asked.

Cat unhooked his seat belt. "I'm good."

"Nervous?"

"A little. But not too bad."

"Have you thought about what you'll do if we don't see him today?"

Cat frowned. "Yeah… I think I'll just let it go for a while. Maybe I'll try to find him in a few months or something."

Porter nodded. There were so many people here, there was a good chance they might not see him even if he did show up. It was a crapshoot. But at least Cat would feel like he tried, like they gave it their best shot. And honestly, that might be the most important thing for him right now anyway. Trying was half the battle.

"I think that's smart," he said. "I think it's going to be okay either way."

Cat dug into his pocket and brought out a tattered picture. It looked like it had been folded and unfolded about a hundred times.

He held it up to Porter. "Just so you know, this is what

he looks like."

Porter narrowed his eyes at the picture—at the skinny young man holding a baby on his hip. Even without it, he would've been able to spot Calvin Roberson in a crowd. Not only was Cat his spitting image, but that fiery hair would be visibly burning, even underneath a Stetson.

He nodded. "Ready, Champ?"

"Ready."

They climbed out of the truck into the chilly Montana morning. The smell of cooking food was stronger now, and Porter pulled it into his lungs. From across the parking lot, they could hear the announcer begin listing local sponsors.

Porter rested his hand on the back of Cat's neck, and they headed toward the front gates like they'd known each other a very long time.

Inside the arena, they stood looking up at the bleachers.

"A lot of folks up there," Porter said. "What do you say, Champ? Do you want to sit down, or take a look around?"

Cat frowned. "Let's sit down. Maybe we'll be able to see better from up there."

They made their way up the bleachers and sat down next to an older woman decked out in turquoise jewelry. She turned and smiled, her hoop earrings catching the light.

"Good morning!"

Porter tipped his hat. "Ma'am."

"Did you two get a program? I have an extra if you want."

"We'd appreciate that. Thanks."

He opened it up and ran his index finger down the schedule for the day, then tapped the morning slot and leaned toward Cat. "Looks like horses this morning, yearlings mostly. Then cattle this afternoon. I think your dad would be here for the horses."

Twisting around, Cat craned his neck. "It's so crowded."

That it was. Porter looked around at the sea of cowboy hats. At all the men and women in boots and jeans. If they saw Calvin today, it would definitely be a stroke of luck.

"Are you two here to shop?" the woman next to them asked. "Or just for fun?"

That's a big neither. But Porter wasn't about to go into it with a total stranger. He smiled. "For fun."

"Well, this is the place to be then." She leaned around him to wink at Cat. "Who knows, your dad might just have to buy you a horse today."

"Oh…no," Porter said. "No, I'm not his dad. Just a friend."

She glanced from one of them to the other. "Oh, I'm sorry. You two just look so much alike."

He and Cat stared at each other. Then smiled. They actually didn't look anything alike. But maybe it was the bond between them that she could see.

"That's okay," Cat said. "He's kind of like a bonus dad." He said this evenly, without hesitation.

Porter's chest warmed, and the woman shook her head.

"Well, I knew it had to be something."

Down in the arena, a man in a white cowboy hat led a chestnut filly in, and a collective *ahhh* moved through the crowd.

"Folks," the announcer boomed over the loudspeakers, "our first horse this morning has a lot of potential. Her mama and daddy were both career rodeo, and she's got calf roping in the blood."

People started shooting their cardboard numbers in the air, and the bidding officially began. For a few minutes, Porter just sat there enjoying the sound of the auctioneer's voice. Not as fast as some he'd heard, but at least he could understand what the guy was saying. Cat sat next to him, watching the little filly being led around the ring.

"Do you think she'll get a good home?" he asked, sounding worried.

Porter looked down at him. Cat was so sensitive. The world could be hard on kids like him. When you felt deeply, you hurt deeply, too.

"Well, this is a special auction. Marietta has a lot of rules about the buyers here. It's a place for ranchers, and for people who want to buy a horse for a companion or a working animal. Other kinds of buyers aren't welcome. It's not like that everywhere, unfortunately, but it is here."

This seemed to satisfy Cat, who sat back and watched the little horse being led out, and another being brought in—this one a brown colt with a white star on his forehead.

They sat there for another hour, scanning the crowd for a cowboy with red hair. For anyone who might look remotely like Cat's father from a distance. People came and went, walking up and down the bleachers with their hot dogs and warm pretzels. Others formed a line below for the bathroom, or a cold beer. But still no Calvin Roberson.

"Hey, Champ," Porter finally said, nudging Cat in the ribs. "Hungry?"

Cat nodded.

"I'm getting cold just sitting here, anyway. Why don't we grab a bite to eat and walk around a little? See what we can see."

"Okay."

They stood and made their way down the bleachers as the auctioneer cried out, "*Sold!* Right there to the fellow in blue!"

The crowd clapped as another horse, the last of the bunch, was brought into the ring. After that, according to the program, it would be cattle for the rest of the afternoon.

Porter stepped down onto the dusty arena floor with Cat behind him. The smell of cooking meat permeated the misty air and his stomach growled. Getting something to eat was a good plan. They'd refuel, get the blood flowing in their legs, and take a look around the other side of the arena.

They got in line for a hot dog, and stood there, shoulders hunched, hands in their pockets. It was obvious that Cat didn't feel like talking, and Porter wasn't going to push.

He'd talk when he was ready. Maybe later they'd head back to the ranch and go for a horseback ride. That might get him talking. Or at the very least, in a better head space to be able to process the day.

The line moved up, and Porter looked around. They had a better vantage point down here. From their spot in line, he could not only see into the arena, but also the covered pens where the horses and cattle were being kept. Dust rose from dozens of hooves pacing nervously back and forth. Cowboys stood at the gates, some leaning against the splintering wood, and some milling about, talking and laughing in small groups.

Porter narrowed his eyes at them, trying to see anything familiar, anyone that looked like the man in the creased picture Cat had tucked inside his pocket.

Cat was looking over, too. Taking it all in.

The line moved up and they moved with it. "What sounds good?" Porter asked. "Those nachos look pretty amazing."

If Cat heard him, he didn't let on. Instead, he kept staring over at the pens where the cattle huffed and pawed at the dirt, their breath rolling from their noses in clouds of silver.

Porter followed his gaze. "What?"

"There," Cat said, his voice hoarse. "Over by the gate closest to us. You see that guy in the green jacket?"

There, where Cat pointed, was a man who had his back turned. He was leaning with his elbows on the fence, one boot on the lowest slat. Another guy was talking to him, pointing out a particular steer in the herd. The man in the green jacket nodded and pushed his Stetson up on his forehead to reveal a shock of flaming-red hair.

Porter heard Cat pull in a breath. His own heartbeat kicked up a notch. An unmistakable physical reaction to what had started out as a purely emotional outing. A day where a son might find his father again. And might find out answers to questions he wasn't really ready to ask.

Porter studied the man from behind. They were too far away to be able to tell for sure…

Cat fidgeted, shifting from foot to foot. "It looks like him."

Porter knew he hadn't seen his father in a long time. It was possible Cat *wanted* it to look like him. But this was exactly why they were here. It was the moment they'd all been anticipating for weeks.

"Should we go over and take a closer look?" Porter asked.

Cat swallowed visibly. Then nodded.

They stepped out of the food line—the thought of eating, now turning Porter's stomach.

They walked side by side, but as they got closer to the pens, Porter shortened his strides. It was hard to know exactly how much support to offer. He wanted Cat to know that he was here for him, but he didn't want his presence to interfere, either. This was Cat's moment. And it was delicate as a spider's web.

They came to a stop a few yards away from the man in green. He was still standing with his back to them, his cream-colored cowboy hat pulled low over his eyes. His shoulders were hunched as he studied the cattle. He was alone now, the man he was talking to before swallowed up by the crowd. It was the perfect time to approach him, if that's what Cat decided to do.

Porter put his hand on Cat's shoulder and squeezed gently. "What do you think, Champ?"

Cat didn't take his eyes off the man in green. It was like they were glued there, watching for any sign of familiarity, anything that would bring back a memory or two. Porter thought back to sitting in that Italian restaurant with Justine, waiting for his mother. He knew how hard Cat's heart was beating inside his chest. He knew how dry his throat was, how his tongue felt like cotton in his mouth. But most of all, he knew all about the doubts that were racing through his mind at that moment. What had he done wrong? Why hadn't he been good enough? If his own father didn't care enough to stick around, who else would?

Porter ground his teeth together, feeling the muscles in his jaw bunch almost painfully. He took his hand off Cat's shoulder and took a small step back. "Whatever happens," he said, his voice low, "I'll be right here, okay?"

Cat looked up at him, his eyes bright. He opened his mouth to say something, and then closed it again. It was entirely possible he didn't know *what* to say, and Porter understood that, too.

Looking back at the man in green, Cat squared his small shoulders. Then took a breath and stepped forward.

The auctioneer's voice boomed from the arena to their right, and the temperature seemed to have dropped in the last few minutes. The tips of Porter's ears felt numb, his fingers tingling inside his jacket pockets. It felt like the world around them had receded, and it was just the boy approaching the man who might be his father. Porter watched with his heart in his throat.

Cat came to a stop behind the man in green. Then reached out and tapped him on the shoulder.

Still holding onto the fence, the man turned just enough to look down at the boy behind him. His cowboy hat sat so low, Porter could barely see his face. Just the shadowy lower half of his jaw, peppered with rusty stubble. A hard mouth. Fair skin that had seen far too much sun over the years.

Cat stared up at him.

And then, the man grew still. His mouth dropped slightly, his expression going slack. Slowly, very slowly, he turned the rest of the way, until he was facing the boy in front of him. In the distance, the auctioneer bellowed a *sold!* that reverberated over the fairgrounds. But the man and boy didn't seem to hear. They just watched each other, oblivious to the people around them. Of the sights and sounds and smells of the auction. For a moment, it was just the two of them.

"Tommy?" The man's voice was low, uncertain.

Porter could see his face now, his eyes, that were unmistakably Cat's. Or Cat's, that were unmistakably his. There was a look of shock in them, utter disbelief.

Even though Cat had planned on coming today, and even though he'd known this moment might happen, it was clear that he hadn't believed it with his whole heart. Probably, he'd been protecting it. Telling himself that either way, he'd be fine. He'd be okay.

But now, here he was. Looking into his dad's face. A face that looked so much like his own.

Porter stood there with his hands in his pockets. He balled them into fists, trying to remember what it felt like to be eleven years old and missing his mother. He'd been wrong before. This moment was much more delicate than a spider's web. It was the dewdrop that hung precariously on its strands.

Cat took a step forward. He had to tilt his head back to see into his father's face. Calvin wasn't a big guy, but he was tall enough. He was tough and wiry, like his son. He also looked like he was at a complete loss for words. Luckily for him, Cat spoke first.

"It's me, Dad. It's Cat."

"Cat..."

"That's what everyone calls me."

Calvin Roberson blinked. The sun had poked through the misty clouds above, and the golden afternoon light slanted across his face.

"What the hell?" Calvin glanced around. "Are you with your grandma?"

"Grandma is in Missoula. She's been sick." Cat said this evenly, and with an unmistakable tone that said Calvin should've already known about Nola's health. "She sent me to Marietta to stay with one of her friends. I'm going to school here and taking horseback riding lessons out at Diamond in the Rough. I'm here with my friend Porter. He owns the ranch."

Calvin glanced over at Porter, before looking down at his son again.

"I heard you might be here," Cat went on, "so I asked him to bring me."

"I don't..." Calvin shook his head. He hooked his thumbs in his belt loops, and then dropped his hands to his sides. "I don't know what to say."

Porter watched this with his head down, his hat pulled low. It was the worst kind of awkward, this painful slowing of time, where there was nothing to do but wait for the older man to reply. With what, Porter didn't know. What *could* he say? What could he possibly come up with to appease his son whom he'd abandoned? Maybe there was nothing to say. Maybe there was only this terrible silence as the auctioneer called over the speakers, and the sun retreated back into the clouds again. Taking with it its temporary warmth. Its temporary hope.

Cat took an obvious breath. Even from where Porter stood, he could see the boy was shaking. Swaying back and forth on his thin legs.

"Why'd you leave?" Cat asked.

Well, then. The kid wasn't going to beat around the bush. He was going to get right down to it, and to hell with making small talk to make anyone feel more comfortable with their shitty decisions.

"Why'd you leave after my mom died?" Cat continued. "Why?"

Porter felt the sharp edges of that question slice his heart. He let his gaze settle on Calvin, who looked like he was feeling it, too. His mouth settled into an expressionless line, his eyes growing distant and cool. His shoulders stiffened, and he leaned away. Almost as if he were afraid to get too close to Cat.

He glanced around, as if expecting someone to intervene. To save him from having to answer.

When he looked back down at Cat, he reminded Porter of a wild horse that had finally accepted its captivity. Nowhere to run. Nowhere to go.

Calvin rubbed his stubbled chin, and then answered in a low tone. "I wasn't any good for your mama, and I wasn't any good for you. You were better off without me, Tommy, believe me."

Cat raised his chin. Porter recognized the fire there. He wondered if this other man would recognize it, too. Be proud of how courageous his son was.

"I don't believe you," Cat said. "I would've liked it better if you'd stayed."

Calvin glanced around again. Maybe worried someone might hear. Worried he'd look like a deadbeat dad. Which he absolutely was.

Porter narrowed his eyes at him, waiting for his answer.

"Aren't you gonna ask about Grandma?" Cat said. His chin, which he'd jutted into the air a second ago, was now starting to tremble. But his eyes flashed. With that same anger Porter had seen the day of the field trip. The day he'd tackled that kid who'd mentioned his parents. Or lack of parents. It had been there ever since, waiting for the right time to claw its way out.

"Shit, son," Calvin said, shaking his head. "Give me a minute to wrap my head around this."

"I don't think you should call me son. I think you should call me Cat."

Calvin stared down at him, clearly not prepared for this. Not prepared for the moment. And sure as hell not prepared for the kid himself.

"Did you know that I always wanted to rodeo like you?" Cat asked flatly.

"No. I didn't."

"I do," Cat finished, his voice suddenly hoarse.

At that, Calvin's expression softened some. He reached out and touched Cat's shoulder. "I'm sure you're different from your old man. And that's a good thing. Rodeo is a hard life. Bull riding hasn't done a whole hell of a lot for me, other than break some bones."

The mist was starting to turn into a light rain, and Porter pulled his collar up against the chill. He didn't take his eyes off Cat, feeling protective, but knowing there wasn't much he could do, either. It was just going to have to play out. A bell that couldn't be unrung.

"If you don't like bull riding, then why are you doing it?" Cat asked.

"I never said I didn't like it."

"You like it more than me."

"Well, now. I never said that, either."

"But you left to rodeo."

Calvin shifted on his feet, clearly uncomfortable. "I left because I would've been a crap dad. I was too young for it. I didn't know how to take care of you…"

It was a terrible excuse, and they both knew it.

"You could come back, you know," Cat said. "Grandma is getting better, and Justine is leaving for a job in England pretty soon. I could come live with you. We could start over."

Porter swallowed hard. Cat had just opened up his bruised and battered heart, and invited his father right in. Not knowing how it would end. Wanting him in his life so much, that he was willing to suffer the consequences, whatever they might be.

It was so brave, that the only thing Porter could picture right then, was Justine's beautiful face that night at the hotel. How she might've reacted if he'd been able to do the same. Where they might be today. Trusting each other with a relationship, even though it was scary as hell? There was no way to know, because he'd chosen the easy way out. The way with the least amount of risk, which is what he'd always done. Every single time.

Porter took his hat off and ran his hand through his hair. The rain was coming harder now, pelting the back of his neck in tiny, stinging drops.

Calvin looked down at his son. What could he say? That he was suddenly going to raise him? It was unrealistic and totally unlikely to happen. Cat probably knew it, but nevertheless, he stood there with his feet planted stubbornly apart, like he was willing himself not to run away. He was waiting for his answer. A hypothetical that he'd been holding onto for a long time now.

Calvin finally shook his head, the rain pattering against his army-green jacket. Tapping against his cowboy hat that concealed so much of his eyes.

"I can't do that, Tommy," he said.

Cat's face crumpled. "Why not?"

"It's complicated."

"What's complicated about it? I'm your kid."

"I know that, and God knows I'll have to live with you hating me for it."

"I don't hate you."

"You should."

"But I don't!"

Calvin's jaw bunched, and he took a deliberate step back. He shook his head in the rain. "I'm sorry, Tommy."

I'm sorry… How many times had Cat heard that before? Probably too many to count.

"My name is Cat." He turned and stumbled past Porter. "I'll be in the truck."

Both men stood there, watching him disappear into the crowd. Physically small for his age, but larger than life where it really mattered.

Porter looked over at Calvin, then stepped forward until he was only a few feet away. His heart thundered in his chest, and he worried for a second that he might actually punch the guy. Did he have *any* idea how special his son was? How much he adored him? It wasn't right that someone should have that much power simply by sharing DNA. Calvin Roberson didn't deserve Cat. He didn't deserve that adoration or that unflinching loyalty. He didn't deserve any of it.

Porter grit his teeth and took an even breath. Calvin watched him warily.

"I'd say it's none of my damn business," Porter said, his voice low, "but that's not true anymore. I've gotten to know that boy, and he's a fine young man. Not that you had anything to do with it. I'll just tell you, though. Think long and hard before you throw him away. The time might come when you're old as shit, and you might want your son around. You might figure out how lucky you were to have him. And by then he'll be gone."

Calvin's jaw bunch and relaxed. He said nothing. Which was wise, since Porter still hadn't decided against punching him.

Pulling his Stetson low, Porter gave him one more look. Then turned toward the parking lot, and the boy with the broken heart.

Chapter Eighteen

PORTER PUT HIS blinker on and turned onto the ranch's bumpy gravel drive. It was raining in earnest now, cold hard drops that splattered relentlessly against the truck's windshield. The wipers couldn't clear it fast enough, moving back and forth in a rubbery rhythm.

Cat sat still, looking out his window. His breath kept fogging it up, and he'd reach up every now and then to rub a clear spot in the glass.

Porter wondered if there was anything he could say to make him feel better. Probably not. He'd probably feel like garbage no matter what, but still…

He licked his lips and took a breath. But Cat turned to him before he could form a word.

"I wasn't planning on asking him to come back," he said quietly. "It just happened."

"You said exactly what you needed to, Champ."

Cat nodded. "It was weird, though. How he acted. I thought he'd want to see me again. I mean, at least a little. But he didn't even seem to care when I told him I wanted to rodeo."

Porter frowned. "I don't think your dad knows what he wants, Cat. Some men are like that. They never really grow up. Even when they're old, they still can't figure it out."

"Your mom is like that, too. Isn't she?"

"Yes, son. She is."

"She could be hanging out at the ranch right this second, getting to know you and Brooks and Griffin. And eating Daisy's food, and riding the horses, and playing with the animals…"

Porter tried to picture his mother, who'd proven herself to be fairly coldhearted, playing with the animals. Maybe that's exactly what she needed. Ranch therapy.

"Instead," Cat continued, "she turned out to be lame."

"I'll agree with that. She is kind of lame."

"Not kind of. *Super* lame."

"Okay. Super lame."

"And that's exactly what my dad is. Super freaking lame."

Porter couldn't argue with this. So he didn't. Instead, he looked over at Cat again and saw that he was glowering underneath his baseball cap. Scowling at the view outside the window with his hands fisted in his lap.

"I don't care if I ever see him again," he said. "Ever."

"Hey, Champ."

Cat only turned farther away, hiding his face.

"I know it's hard to believe right now," Porter said, "but you might feel differently later. After you've grown up a little. You might have a different view of things."

"You waited until you were grown-up to find your mom, and it turned out the same. It doesn't matter how old I get. My dad is always gonna suck."

"But maybe not..." Porter could hardly believe he was defending the guy. Or at least, trying to convince Cat that he might change with time. But he couldn't stand the bitterness in the kid's voice. The finality of his tone. He'd felt like that once. And it had nearly eaten him alive.

"I'm not sorry I found my mom, Cat," he said. The truck bounced over a pothole, and they rocked from side to side. "Remember how you told me I'd feel better if I tried? I do feel better. I know a lot more now than I did. But that doesn't mean I won't try again in the future. As mad as I am at her, and as mad as I know you are at your dad, it doesn't mean they can't change. That we can't give them the time and grace to be better people."

"I just wish I could make him *feel* something," Cat said. "I wish I could make him feel bad for leaving. I don't even think he feels bad."

"Trust me. He feels bad. I think he's just terrible at showing it."

Cat glared out the window as the ranch came into view, blurred by the steady rain. It was gray and cold, Thanksgiving only a week away.

Porter put the truck into park as Clifford came running from underneath the porch. His black and white fur was immediately soaked, making him look more like a wet mop than a border collie. He waited outside the passenger-side door for Cat to step out, quivering on his hind quarters.

"That dog worships the ground you walk on," Porter said. "I think he likes you better than me at this point."

That got a small smile from Cat, as he opened the door. Clifford immediately began wiggling at his feet.

He turned to Porter, the rain tapping on his shoulders. "Can I go see Abby and Wookiee before Justine comes to pick me up?"

At the mention of Justine's name, Porter's chest tightened. He'd been trying hard not to admit that he missed her so much. Very damn hard. But it was becoming more and more clear that no matter how hard he tried, he was still going to feel the loss her of, the loss of the possibility of her, acutely.

"Sure," he said. "You can give them some grain. They haven't had any today."

Cat nodded.

"And Champ?"

"Yeah?"

"Be careful. This mud is making things dangerous. I almost broke my neck in one of the turnouts yesterday."

"Okay."

Cat pushed the door closed, and Porter watched him walk through the rain with the little dog at his side. They looked like a picture, a painting of the American West.

Again, Porter's chest tightened, but this time it didn't have anything to do with Justine, and had everything to do with this kid who'd come into his life and turned it upside down. He didn't really know how he was going to say goodbye to Cat. But more than that, he didn't understand why he should have to. He belonged in Marietta. And so did Justine, whether she knew it or not.

Porter sat there for a minute with the rain beating on the truck's roof. It was coming harder now, relentlessly, and he knew that in a few weeks, as the temperature continued to drop, Diamond in the Rough would be blanketed in snow. And this time, it would probably stick around until spring. And where would they all be by then? He and Cat and Justine? Divided by imaginary walls that didn't make much sense? Or would someone come to their senses and say what needed to be said? Even if the answers weren't necessarily clear. It would take some faith, Porter realized with a heavy feeling in his stomach. It would take faith, and it would take courage.

He looked over at the barn and felt the muscles in his jaw tighten. He could see Alloy in his turnout, standing in the rain like a shadow. Big and bulky and still.

And then the bull lifted his head. Looking toward something that was hidden from Porter's view.

Slowly, the animal lumbered out of sight. Normally it took an act of God, or at least an apple or two, to get him to move. Cat was probably tempting him with something, calling him over for a pat. He loved that damn bull, drawn to him because of the rodeo, or his dad, or who knew what.

Porter suddenly stiffened. He thought of the look in Cat's eyes a few minutes before, the set of his mouth. Hurt, angry. So incredibly angry…

Uneasy, he reached for the door and opened it into the rain.

Just as a scream pierced the air.

His heart dropped into his stomach, but he didn't give himself time to think. He ran toward the turnout, mud splashing underneath his boots. From the other side of the barn, Clifford was barking frantically. And then there was moaning. Faint, but the sound sent a chill all the way to Porter's scalp.

He tore around Alloy's turnout fence, sliding on the wet grass. Righting himself, he looked up to see Clifford standing over Cat in the turnout. The boy was lying in the fetal position, holding his arm to his stomach. Alloy stood a few feet away, quivering and pawing at the mud.

Porter slowed, watching the bull warily from the corner of his eye. Feeling sick as the realization of what just happened, of what *could've* happened, sunk in. "It's alright, big guy. Just calm down…"

Alloy snorted and shook his blocky head. Water and bull slobber went flying. But he stayed put. Thank God.

"*Ooohhh.*"

This from Cat, whose face was twisted in pain.

Heart pounding, Porter knelt down and brushed his mop of red hair away from a goose egg on his forehead. Then began looking for any other injuries.

"My arm," Cat said, his voice hoarse.

"I know, Champ," Porter said. "Just hold still." He scooped the boy up in his arms, careful not to slip in the mud. Clifford ran around them in circles, beside himself.

"It's okay. We're going to get you to the hospital now. It's gonna be alright."

Cat's head tipped against Porter's chest. He barely weighed anything at all. "I just wanted to feel…" His small voice trailed off.

Before he passed clean out.

JUSTINE SAT AT her kitchen table with a pile of monthly bills, unable to concentrate on any of them. The rain tapped against the window over the sink in a steady cadence that was lulling her into a midafternoon stupor. She'd rather be curled up on the couch with a cup of tea and a book, than paying bills.

She sighed. It needed to be done. And besides, she knew if she let herself sit down on the couch, what she'd really be doing would be giving in to obsessing about the livestock auction. Cat had texted when they'd gotten there, but she hadn't heard from him since. She'd resisted the urge to text

Porter, not wanting to seem needy, which she absolutely was. Even though she didn't have a claim to either one of them, these were her guys. And it felt strange to be apart from them right now. On this day that would dredge up so many feelings for Cat. And Porter, too.

When it came right down to it, she couldn't concentrate on her electric bill, or how many gallons of water she'd used this month. And she really didn't care. Which wasn't like her at all.

Putting her pen down, she took off her glasses and rubbed her eyes. Pretty soon this little house would belong to someone else. She hadn't been here that long, but she'd managed to fall in love with it just the same.

She looked around, feeling her heart thump against her rib cage. With her landlord's blessing, she and Jemma had painted the living room and bedrooms on the weekend she'd moved in. Her dad had come over to put new fixtures in the bathroom, cute little faucet handles that reminded her of antiques, and that fit the character of the space perfectly.

Just like she felt that Porter and Cat were hers somehow, she felt like this house was hers. Even though her name wasn't on the title, she felt a connection to it. Especially right then, with the rain tapping against the single-paned windows, and the wind chimes tinkling on the porch.

Putting her glasses back on, she picked up her gas bill and tried pushing the acute feeling of loss away to the farthest corners of her mind. But it lingered there anyway, pulling at her heart, making her swallow the sudden lump in her throat. Just because she felt like something was hers, didn't make it hers. Didn't make *them* hers. Not unless she wanted to take a chance for once in her life.

From the kitchen counter, her phone rang. Standing up, she padded over in her slippers and picked it up. *Porter…*

She smiled. "Hello?"

"Justine?"

The reception was crackly and hollow. It sounded like he was driving.

"Porter, hey. How's it going?"

"Cat…we're…into town…"

He was cutting out.

Frowning now, she switched the phone to her other ear. "What? I didn't get that."

"…storm…cell…"

"What?"

"There was…accident…but hospital…"

Her heart stopped. Did he say *hospital*?

"Can you meet…there?"

"Marietta General?"

And then he was gone. The call dropped. She stood there for a second with her blood rushing in her ears.

Then grabbed her coat and purse and ran out the door.

Chapter Nineteen

JUSTINE WALKED DOWN the hallway at Marietta General, conscious of the shining waxed floor underneath her feet, of the disinfectant smell that permeated the air. Of the sound of doctors being paged overhead, and the orderlies talking in low tones at the nurse's station to her left. But all she could think about was Cat. *Cat, Cat, Cat…*

His name kept repeating inside her head. She felt like if she concentrated on it enough, she wouldn't be able to picture what had happened at the ranch. How desperate he must've been. A clear cry for help that had knocked the breath out of all of them.

All this time, she thought he'd been ready to try and connect with his dad again. But in reality, seeing Calvin today had been more than he could handle. It had triggered something that he hadn't been equipped to deal with. She hadn't seen it. Neither had Porter.

When she'd finally reached him on the way to the hospital, he'd had a hard time telling her what had happened. It was clear that he felt responsible, but the truth was, they were all responsible. But no more than Calvin Roberson himself, who'd walked out years ago, leaving his only son with issues he'd most likely struggle with his entire life.

Swallowing hard, she turned a corner to see the waiting room up ahead. Even with everything that had happened in his young life so far, Justine knew that Cat would be okay. Eventually, this pain would ebb, and he'd be able to see things more clearly. He'd be able to see how amazing he was, and that he wasn't to blame for any of this. Not for his mom dying, and not for his father walking out. Those were things that had happened to him. They didn't define him. It was a lesson she'd come to learn, too. Especially over this last year. Her time in Marietta had taught her how beautiful life could be if you just let go of all the dark things getting in the way. Porter had been a point of light for her. And so had Cat.

She slowed as she entered the waiting room and looked around. There was a woman sitting in the corner with a little girl on her lap. An older gentleman filling up his coffee cup, who looked exhausted. There was a nurse talking to a young couple a few feet away, and there, by the window, was Porter. Standing tall and still, gazing out onto the rainy parking lot with a grim tilt to his mouth. He wasn't wearing his Stetson, but it had left its trademark ring around his dark hair. A country halo, and to her, it couldn't have been more fitting.

She walked up behind him and wrapped her arms around his waist.

Startling, he turned, then smiled and pulled her against

his chest.

"I'm so glad you're here," he said quietly. "Brooks is holding down the fort at the ranch, and Griffin has some clients that he can't leave just yet. But really, you're the only person I wanted to see anyway."

"Same," she said, breathing in his warm scent. Feeling his heart beat against her cheek. "I couldn't get here fast enough." She pulled away enough to look up at him. "How is he?"

Porter frowned. "He has a greenstick fracture in his right arm. I had to ask what the hell that was, I had no idea. It's a break, but not broken in half. And he has a pretty nasty bump on the head. They're setting his arm now."

"Oh my God."

"Yeah. But it could've been a lot worse. A whole hell of a lot worse."

As he said it, her stomach twisted. Then it all started playing like a grainy movie inside her head. She pictured Cat calling Alloy over to the fence. Climbing up on it and waiting until the bull was close enough to touch. Then swinging his leg over the back of the massive, muddy animal, and holding on for dear life.

They wouldn't know what he'd been thinking until they had a chance to talk to him. But it was obvious this had been about his father. All of his suffering had simply reached a boiling point.

Justine felt her eyes fill with tears. Before she could help it, they rolled down her cheeks, one after the other. It was as if someone had turned on a faucet, with all the emotion from the last few weeks finally being set free. All this time, ever since her father had left her mother, she'd been careful with letting herself feel too much. Hurt too much. Love too much.

But now, standing here in a man's arms whom she absolutely knew she loved, she was tired of fighting it. Tired of feeling like she was holding back the tide. She just wanted to let it come, bringing with it all the things she'd been denying herself for years. Because along with potential pain, came potential happiness. Contentment. And joy.

"Hey, hey, hey," Porter said. He brushed his thumb underneath her bottom lashes. "What's wrong?"

"I'm sorry. I don't know where this is coming from." That was a lie. Yes, she did. She just wasn't being open with him, honest with him, which needed to be the first step.

"Well," she tried again. "That's not exactly true..."

He lifted his brows. His eyes were so dark right then, they reminded her of water at midnight. Beautiful, reflective pools of green. The effect was pure and absolute. Her heart beat painfully inside her chest as she struggled to find the words to describe how she was feeling. And what it was she really wanted.

She stepped back, knowing that in order to say what she needed to, she was going to have to do it without his arms around her. She needed this to be scary. She needed to put something on the line here, in order for it to mean what it should.

Clasping her hands in front of her belly, she took a steadying breath. It seemed like she couldn't get enough oxygen into her lungs. It just floated over them in an invisible cloud, leaving her shaking and breathless.

"I thought I had it all figured out," she said, her voice low. "Before I moved to Marietta. Before Cat came to stay with me. Before I met you."

He gazed down at her, his jaw working. But he stayed quiet, waiting for her to go on.

"I've spent so much time running away from life, that I honestly think I've forgotten how to live it," she continued. "Going to England, that's been a dream of mine ever since I can remember, but—"

"I'm going to stop you right there."

She looked up at him questioningly.

"I need to interrupt you," he said, "because I should say this before you get anything else out. No matter what it is you're about to say."

"Okay…" She waited, every nerve ending in her body jumping.

"I should've told you this a while ago. I should've told you that night in the hotel, but I didn't know how to without scaring the hell out of you. And scaring the hell out of me to be completely honest. But this morning at the auction, it just hit me." He paused. Then cleared his throat before going on. "I watched while Cat was so damn brave. He was so brave, and I realized I've just been… Well, I've been chickenshit," he said evenly.

She felt the corners of her mouth tilt at that.

"I found my mom," he continued. "And that was good, I guess. Because that was about me starting to open the door to people… But then she didn't show, and I just ended up closing it again." He smiled down at her. "Do you see where I'm going with this?"

"I think I do. I hope I do."

He looked over as a doctor walked past. Justine's stomach curled into a tight little knot as she thought of Cat's broken arm. As she absorbed everything Porter was saying. It was almost too much, and she felt her knees begin to shake underneath her.

Porter looked back down at her. Then reached for her hand. He rubbed her knuckles with his thumb, and it was almost like he was massaging her heart instead. How she ever thought she could deny herself his touch without at least fighting for it first, was beyond her comprehension. It was time to fight like hell.

"Porter," she began. "I need to tell you something."

"Okay. But first I want to ask you to stay…"

She stared up at him.

"Yeah," he said. "I should've asked after that first kiss. Because that's when I think I knew."

The knot in her stomach eased. And then there were butterflies. What felt like dozens and dozens of them, brushing up against her rib cage with their velvety wings.

He wanted her to stay. He'd actually said it. Even though he had no idea if they'd even work as a couple. Even though he wasn't sure how she felt, he'd taken the chance. He'd taken the chance on *her*.

He pulled her closer, until her hips rubbed up against his belt buckle. It was cold and rigid, and the feel of it through her clothes was surprisingly erotic.

"The thing is, Justine," he said, "that I'm in love with you. And I think you belong here in Marietta. With me."

She loved those words. She wanted to soak them in. Let them fill her to the brim.

"I think you might be right," she said quietly.

He watched her; his big hand splayed across her lower back.

"And what I wanted to tell you," she said, "is that I'm going to cancel my trip." She found that her voice was shaking right along with her knees. But not with apprehension. With joy. She'd wanted this all along. She hadn't wanted to leave. She'd been wanting to stay.

"It's early enough that they'll be able to get someone else," she continued. "I'll end up going eventually, but not to run away from something. To run toward it. That's how it should be, right?"

Porter smiled. Sexy crinkles radiated from the corners of his eyes; dimples cut into each stubbled cheek. He was gorgeous. And she realized at that moment, that he could eventually be hers. If things worked out the way she hoped they might.

"And I want to ask Nola if I can keep Cat through high school," she finished. "I want to help her raise him in Marietta. If that's what he wants, too."

Porter pulled in a breath and turned to look out the window. When he exhaled, she felt some of the tension go out of his body. Tension she hadn't realized had been there until right then.

When he turned back at her, there was something in his eyes that she recognized instantly. She recognized it because she was feeling it, too. It was relief.

"Well," he said, in his low drawl. "I was hoping you'd say that."

"You were?"

"Yeah. And it's convenient, too, because now I don't have to haul you both over my shoulder to keep you here."

She laughed, leaning into him.

"Seriously, though," he said, his smile fading a little. "Nobody has ever put anything on the line for me before. Not like this. And I'd bet Cat feels the same."

"I just hope…I just hope he'll want to stay. Nola and I talked about it the other day. Hypothetically. She wants whatever will make him happiest, and so do I. We just have to figure out what that is."

"The most important thing is that he'll have a choice.

Which he hasn't had in a while."

She nodded at that. It was the truth. He'd been denied the one thing that might've made him feel more in control all this time. It couldn't have been helped, though. Nola had done the best she could. Justine had tried her best, too. But now, with her decision not to take this job, so many more doors would be open to Cat that hadn't been before. The thought made her heart happy.

They stood there in each other's arms. Porter rested his chin on the top of her head, and she lay her cheek against his chest. She stared out the window to the parking lot, to the rain pattering against the window, to the soft, gauzy clouds cloaking the blue mountains in the distance. It was the prettiest she'd ever seen Marietta look.

She exhaled softly. Or maybe it was just the fact that she felt more at home here now than ever before. She realized then how lucky she was. She'd reconciled with her dad—a huge step toward healing that she'd been needing to take for a long time. She had her sister, whom she adored. She had her little house, a job that she loved. And now, she had the possibility of a new love story. Her love story. It was more than she'd ever hoped for.

"Mr. Cole?"

They both turned at the sound of the voice behind them. There, standing a few feet away was a nurse in pink scrubs.

"Yes?" Porter said.

"Cat is in recovery. He's a little groggy, but you can see

him now."

JUSTINE SAT BESIDE the hospital bed, watching Cat begin to open his eyes. His lids would flutter momentarily, and then close again, his lashes strawberry-blond smudges against his freckled cheeks.

His arm was tucked securely beside him, wrapped in a blue cast. The bump on his head was in the process of turning purple, but by tomorrow morning it would be black and blue. But other than those two things, and some dried mud in his hair, he looked perfectly fine. Not a scratch on him, which, under the circumstances, was a miracle.

Justine looked over at Porter, who was standing by the window. He stared down at Cat, his jaw working. She knew what he was thinking, because she was thinking it, too. *Thank God.* Thank God it wasn't any worse.

Cat moaned softly and opened his eyes again. Before Justine could reach out to take his hand, his chin began trembling.

"Hey," she whispered. "It's okay."

Porter pulled a chair up to the bed. "It's alright, Champ."

"I'm sorry," he said. "I'm so sorry."

"Hey, now." Porter leaned closer and tweaked his nose. "You probably gave Alloy the thrill of his life. You can only stand in a pasture eating apples for so long before you start getting a little bored, right? And who knows, maybe he's destined to be a rodeo bull after all."

Cat's face crumpled. "You're not mad at him, are you? It wasn't his fault."

"No, he was only doing what bulls do. It confused him is all. But he's so big. We're just lucky he didn't step on you when you fell off."

"I know," he said, his eyes filling with tears. "I wasn't planning on doing it. It just…kind of happened. He got so close to the fence, and I wanted to see what it felt like. To be my dad for just a second."

Porter and Justine looked at each other. Her heart beat slowly, painfully, and with each beat, she could feel her blood whoosh through her veins. *Poor Cat.* Poor, sweet little kid, who only wanted his father in his life.

He was in so much pain. Emotional pain, and now physical pain, too… It was such a tangled web, that Justine knew it would be hard to work him free. But if he stayed with her in Marietta, if he could keep spending time at the ranch, she felt like they'd be heading in the right direction.

Cat reached up and wiped his cheeks with his free hand. "I guess this means you're not gonna trust me around the animals anymore, right?"

Porter frowned. "That's not what it means at all. You made a mistake. You paid a price, and you learned from it. I trust you, Champ."

This kindness didn't seem to be what Cat expected, because he started crying in earnest then—big, hiccupping sobs that broke Justine's heart.

"Hey." Porter handed him a tissue from the box next to the bed. "You had a jolt today, kiddo. Several jolts, actually. It's going to be okay. Justine and I are here for you no matter what. We care about you, and we're not going anywhere."

"But Justine is," Cat said, his voice cracking. "She's leaving and I'll be leaving, and I'll miss it here so much." He looked over at Justine miserably. "I'm sorry. I never wanted to make you feel bad for leaving. And I don't want to hurt my grandma's feelings. She doesn't have anybody but me, and I need to go back and be with her, but...but..." He let his voice trail off, as the tears streamed down his face.

Justine reached for his hand again. "What would you say if I didn't leave, Cat?"

He gazed up at her. "What?"

"How would you feel if I decided to stay?"

"Because of me? Because I'm crying like a baby?"

She laughed. "No. Because I want to stay."

He stared at her, his mouth hanging open.

"Life is short, buddy," she continued. "I don't want to miss out on the things that make me the happiest. And I've realized that *you* make me happy. Having you live with me makes me happy. Getting to spend time at the ranch with Porter, that makes me happy, too."

"But what about London? I know you were excited to

go."

"I was. And I am. I'll go, but not right now. And if I'm lucky, I'll still have a job at Marietta Middle next year. Maybe not teaching the same grade, but close…"

He blinked at her. "So you might stay…and I might get to come visit after I go back to Missoula?"

"Well, here's the thing…" She glanced over at Porter, who was looking back. "I was thinking you might stay with me. For as long as you wanted. Through high school, maybe. Until you graduate."

"For *good*?"

"Well, until graduation." She winked. "And then I'd kick you right out."

He grinned. And then, his expression fell again. "But my grandma…"

"I've already talked to her about this, Cat. She would miss you, for sure. But she knows how much you love it here, and she wants you to be happy. I know you're worried about her being lonely, but she could come visit all the time. I'll have the guest room all made up; it can be all hers. And we can go to Missoula to see her, too. Every weekend, if you want."

He seemed to consider this.

Justine squeezed his hand. "Your grandma is getting better. She's loved raising you—you've been the joy of her life. I know it's hard to think about it this way, honey, but she could also use some time now for herself. To do the things she's always wanted to do."

Cat raised his brows, clearly not having thought of this before. "Like what?"

"Well, I know she's been wanting to travel. To join some clubs. And you know how she's always talked about getting a tiny house? She was even thinking of buying one, and some property with a view. Having you here would give her some freedom that she hasn't had in a while. I think it might be like giving her a gift in a way. Now that she has her health back, she can have some adventures back, too. Does that make sense?"

He nodded slowly. And then he smiled again. This time, wide and true. "You'd really want me?"

"I'd *really* want you."

Justine's phone buzzed from her pocket, and she let go of Cat's hand to fish it out.

She swiped her thumb over the screen to see a text from Nola. Her stomach dropped. She'd been so focused on getting to the hospital, that she'd forgotten to call her. She'd need to step out in the hallway to explain everything. There was a lot to unpack.

But before she could stand up, she opened the text and read the whole thing.

Leaving a friend's house, no service. Hope this goes through. Calvin just called. He's looking for Cat…

Chapter Twenty

PORTER HUNG UP with Griffin, then looked down at Justine, who was tugging nervously on a strand of dark hair.

"What'd he say?" she asked quietly. They'd left Cat's room a few minutes ago, and were standing in the hallway, so there was no chance he could hear. But it didn't matter, she was in full protective mode. Porter knew if she could, she'd roll Cat up in some Bubble Wrap. He'd had enough shocks for one day.

"After Calvin talked to Nola, he called the ranch. Griffin answered and told him what happened. That we were at the hospital. Calvin hung up before he said anything else, but Griffin got the feeling he was on his way here."

Justine rubbed her temples. "Oh, God. Oh no. Now what?"

"I guess we just wait here to try and intercept him before he sees Cat. Maybe we can get a feeling of what he wants to say."

"I wonder if we should tell Cat he's coming. I just don't want his heart to get any more broken today."

Porter leaned down and kissed her soft lips. Loving the feel of them. And understanding exactly how she felt. He wanted to protect them both.

When he leaned away again, he cupped her face in his hands. "I know. But what if we tell him, and then Calvin doesn't show up? The guy doesn't have a great track record so far."

She nodded. "You're right. I'm just panicking a little."

"You're allowed. I think we're all allowed to be on edge today."

Nurses kept walking past them, looking busy and in charge. A man with a huge bouquet of flowers disappeared into the room next door, and Porter could smell their heavy fragrance from where they stood. All of a sudden, he was bone-tired. His back felt stiff, his legs ached. He guessed the adrenaline from earlier was bound to catch up to him eventually, and he'd barely slept the night before.

Rolling his head from side to side, he resisted the urge to yawn. "I think I'm gonna grab a cup of coffee. Want one?"

"I'd love one, actually."

He looked up at the clock above the nurse's station. "They're probably going to be discharging him soon. Maybe we'll be gone before Calvin gets here…"

"Sorry to disappoint you."

At the sound of the gravelly voice behind them, they both turned.

Calvin Roberson stood there with his hands in his pockets, his cowboy hat pulled low over his eyes. The shoulders of his jacket were soaked with rain, and he looked ragged around the edges. Older than when Porter had seen him earlier in the day, if that was possible. But that probably had everything to do with the expression on his face—a mixture of worry and regret. It was as clear as the clouds hanging low in the Montana sky outside. And just as dark.

Porter had been pissed at him earlier. In fact, it had taken all his strength not to wring the guy's neck at the livestock auction. But standing here now, he looked smaller. Not just bull-rider skinny with the legs to match, but *small.* Beaten down. Even his shoulders were hunched in a way that suggested contrition. And shame.

Justine moved closer to Porter. Together, he knew they probably looked formidable. Putting out all kinds of parental vibes. Literally guarding the door to Cat's hospital room.

Calvin reached up and took off his hat, pinching the brim between his thumb and forefingers. He looked down at his muddy boots for a long moment. His red hair was plastered to his head, a little too shaggy in the back, and brushing the collar of his jacket like a feather. Cat had the same hair. The same freckles. No matter what happened between these two in the future, there was no denying the blood they shared.

"I know what you probably think of me," Calvin said.

They watched him steadily, neither one of them answering. Porter didn't know about Justine, but he wasn't in the business of making dads feel better about leaving their kids. It was true that Calvin deserved some credit for showing up here today, but he was a long way from being let off the hook.

Porter ground his teeth together, waiting.

"I'd think the same thing," Calvin continued. "And I don't expect you to understand, but I was always planning on coming back. When I got on my feet. But a few months led to six, and six months led to a year. And, well…I don't have to spell it out for you, do I?"

No, he didn't.

"I was seventeen when Cat's mama got pregnant," Calvin continued. "Eighteen when he was born. I was a messed-up kid with a really shitty homelife, and I couldn't get used to the idea of being a dad, when all I knew about dads was that they hit you. Told you how dumb you were, how you'd never amount to nothing…until you started believing it."

Porter's shoulders stiffened. He thought of his own mother. How she and Porter's father had struggled with the responsibility of parenthood, until eventually, she'd just run away from it all together. And she'd been grown at the time. And definitely hadn't had an abusive upbringing. Calvin couldn't say either one of those things.

It was a simple explanation, but Porter guessed it might be more than Cat had been offered up until now. All in the name of protecting him. He could relate to that, too. For a long time, his father had made excuses for his mom in order to keep the pain at bay. He'd tried his best, but it had only deepened the wound. He wondered if his dad had been honest with him in the beginning, if he would've been able to reconcile her abandonment as a kid, instead of continuing to wrestle with it as an adult. He'd never know, of course. But he couldn't help but go there, anyway.

"Calvin…" Justine stepped forward, obviously softening. Maybe that was a mistake. Maybe they were the worst kinds of suckers, but Porter didn't think so. Whatever Calvin Roberson's intentions were, he felt like they were witnessing a moment of honesty here. Of vulnerability, from a man who probably wasn't used to dealing in either.

Calvin held up a hand. "Ma'am, I don't know you, but I do know you've been taking care of my boy, and that's reason enough to want forgiveness from you. But I'm not expecting it. I just want you to know why. Why I left, why I stayed away. It was never because I didn't love him. I think it was because I was afraid of loving him too much."

Justine was quiet at that.

"When I saw y'all today," Calvin said, looking over at Porter, "I was so damn shocked, I didn't know what to say. I know I was an asshole. I just needed some time. And then I called Nola, and she told me about the cancer…" He swallowed visibly. "Well, I don't even know what to say to that. She'd have every right never to let me see my kid again."

Justine gave him a small smile. "She wouldn't do that.

She's an amazing person. That doesn't mean she'd take any crap from you, though. Just so you know."

He smiled back. Then looked beyond them into the hospital room where a nurse was checking on Cat.

He took a deep breath. "I have no idea what's gonna happen from here. But I can tell you that I want to see my boy. If you'll allow it."

Porter put an arm around Justine. Wanting her to know that he'd support her, however she decided to handle this. It was complicated. And delicate. And would have lasting consequences, no matter what. But he knew she was up for it. She'd fight for Cat now, just like she had from the beginning.

"You're his dad," she said quietly. "Of course we'll allow it."

Calvin stood there clutching his hat. And Porter could see that his hands were trembling. This man rode fifteen-hundred-pound bulls for a living. But apparently, all it took to bring him to his knees was a little boy who didn't weigh a buck-oh-five soaking wet.

Porter smiled, feeling his reluctant heart expand a little. "He'll be happy to see you," he said. "You two have a lot in common."

Justine leaned into his side, and he thought for the thousandth time, how well she fit there. Like a puzzle piece sliding into place.

Rubbing her arm, he watched Calvin take a deep breath

and then step slowly past them, and into the hospital room where his son was waiting.

Porter looked down at Justine. Her eyes were maybe the deepest blue he'd ever seen. He never would've thought that hospital lighting could make someone look so pretty, but lately he'd been experiencing a lot of firsts.

It was fitting, really. Finding the beauty where there shouldn't be much. But that's what Justine had brought to his life. Beauty and hope. Possibilities in what had been a sea of doubt.

From inside the hospital room, there was a surprised gasp. And then a long, meaningful pause.

"Hi, Dad."

"Hey there, son."

Epilogue

JUSTINE PULLED UP to the ranch house and came to a stop behind her dad's truck.

The sun had finally come out, just in time for Thanksgiving dinner, and as she turned off the engine, she looked around at all the cars in the driveway. It would be a big gathering, but Diamond in the Rough was used to those. Her sister and EJ, her dad and Nancy, Nola, Daisy and Brooks, Griffin and Rae, Eddie and his new girlfriend (a very nice lady named Jill, who wasn't swayed at all by his fame), and of course, his guitar for after dinner entertainment... Plus, the ranch hands and a few other friends who hadn't had any family to spend the holiday with.

Justine gazed up at the porch where Daisy had arranged pumpkins and dried corn stalks by the front door. She took a deep breath, feeling emotional. Gratitude for a whole family. Peace. Love in all its intricate layers, blanketing her heart. It would be a full house. The only person who'd declined an invitation for dinner was Calvin, but he'd promised to be there for dessert. He was still getting used to big family functions, but he was trying. Last year he'd only shown up for coffee. Dessert was progress.

Unbuckling, she turned at the whimpering in the back seat. There in a small crate, was a scruffy black puppy. The shelter staff hadn't been able to tell her what breed he was—most likely too many to count.

He pawed the wire and looked at her through liquid brown eyes.

"Aww, I know sweetheart. You've been such a good boy. Your life is about to change forever, I promise."

The puppy wagged his stubby tail. In fact, his whole bottom wiggled at the sound of her voice.

She laughed. "If anyone would've told me that I'd end up with a dog *and* a Cat, I would've said they were reaching. But here we are, right?"

The puppy gave one joyous yip, right as the front door opened. *Right on time…*

Porter stepped out with his hands planted on the boy's shoulders in front of him. Cat was getting so *tall.* He'd shot up over the summer but hadn't started filling out yet, so he was as skinny as his dad. There was a red bandanna over his eyes, a blindfold that was supposed to keep him from peeking until they were ready.

Grinning, she waved at Porter. She loved surprises. And this was a whopper.

She climbed out of the car and opened the back door, hoping the puppy wouldn't bark again. Then she pulled the crate out and readjusted it underneath her arm. The little dog immediately busied himself with licking her fingers through the wire.

Porter cleared his throat. "I wonder where Justine could be?" he asked in a loud exaggerated voice. "She must've had to…do something," he finished lamely.

She laughed, and there went her cover. But she couldn't help it. It was so cheesy, so utterly *dad*-like, that her entire body hummed with love for him. He was going to be an amazing father. She knew he'd be there when his children fell. He'd kiss their skinned knees and help them right back up again. He would make sure they felt loved and safe, and never, ever alone in this world.

She knew this, because he made her feel like that on a daily basis.

Shifting the crate against her slightly swollen belly, she headed toward the front porch. A cold breeze blew against her cheeks, making them tingle. Her hair was up today, and a few loose strands blew over her face.

She climbed the steps toward Porter and Cat, her little family that had materialized over this last year. An unexpected gift which she gave thanks for every day. But especially today, a holiday that she'd come to believe had brought them together.

Slowly, she came to a stop in front of her guys, with the puppy still working at her fingers through the wire. Sometimes she couldn't believe how lucky she was. How she'd managed this life. This Montana dream come true. But she'd also learned not to question it anymore. She deserved this. She deserved happiness. But most of all, she deserved love.

Porter gazed down at her, giving Cat's shoulders a squeeze. His gold wedding band winked in the late-afternoon sun. A reminder that he was hers, and she was his. Always.

"What the heck?" Cat said, his voice cracking. It did that lately. It made his freckled cheeks blaze with color, but Justine thought it was the sweetest thing she'd ever heard. It meant he was growing. He was thriving. Here in Marietta with her and Porter, where he was going to stay until college. He'd changed his mind about the bull riding for now. Something Calvin had helped convince him of. It wasn't an easy life. And he wanted more for his son.

"Can I take this off now?" Cat smiled. "Justine, I know it's you."

She nodded at Porter, barely able to contain herself.

"Okay, Champ," Porter said. "One, two…*three.*"

He lifted the bandanna off, and Cat blinked into the sunlight. When he saw the puppy, his mouth fell open.

"We wanted it to be a surprise," Justine said. "You and Clifford can show him the ropes."

"He's mine? My own dog?"

"Your very own," Porter said.

Justine set the crate down and bent to open it. The puppy bounded out in a blur of black fur and launched himself directly into Cat's arms.

Laughing, the boy scooped him up. "Thank you! Thank you so much!"

"Hey," Porter said. "You've earned it. Straight As? I mean, come on."

It was obvious Cat only heard half of that. The puppy was squirming in his arms and bathing his face in kisses. This baby of his would be a full-time job. A job that Justine thought everyone should have at least once in their life.

She moved into Porter's side as they watched the boy carry the dog down the steps and plop him down in the yard. They began chasing each other around, with Cat's laughter echoing through the air.

The door opened behind them, and she looked over her shoulder to see Brooks step out onto the porch. Followed by Griffin, who was holding a beer. Both men were watching Cat and the puppy, smiling that signature Cole smile. Rugged but warm, sensitive and knowing. Eddie had it, too. Justine adored that smile.

"I see Elvira's got a new archenemy," Brooks said, slapping Porter on the back. "That puppy better get used to cat claws in his ass."

Porter laughed. "She'd better learn to run faster."

"Justine," Griffin said, "Rae just opened the wine, but she brought you some sparkling cider. Want a glass?"

"Oh, that sounds good. Thank you."

"I'll go get it. Come on, Brooks. You can help with the wine."

Brooks nodded amiably and followed him back inside. The three brothers were always ribbing each other, but when it came right down to it, they worked together seamlessly. Whether it was serving Thanksgiving dinner to a houseful of hungry guests or running a working dude ranch with grit to spare, it was something to behold. A family affair. And now, Justine was a part of that family—a fact that filled her with a quiet, immeasurable joy.

Porter wrapped an arm around her shoulders and pulled her close.

"Well, Cat seems pretty happy, don't you think?"

"I think he seems as happy as I feel," she said softly.

He kissed the top of her head as the sun continued its slow, golden descent toward the mountains in the distance. It would be dark in a few hours, and the country stars would sparkle overhead. The turkey and fixings would be put away, and the pies and coffee would come out, and they'd welcome their very last guest through the doors of the ranch house that she'd come to love so much.

She looked up at Porter just as he rested a big hand on her belly. Where their baby was curled, warm and safe, and loved beyond measure.

"Ready for dinner?" he asked.

She could smell the food from where they stood, and her mouth watered. Beside them in the yard, the puppy growled and tugged on the leg of Cat's jeans. Justine closed her eyes for a minute, soaking it all in. Not wanting to forget a single minute of this day. Not wanting to take any of it for granted.

Before she could open them again, she felt Porter's lips on hers.

And her heart was full.

The End

Want more? Check out Brooks and Daisy's story in *Montana Rancher's Kiss*!

Join Tule Publishing's newsletter for more great reads and weekly deals!

If you enjoyed *The Montana Cowboy's Heart,*
you'll love the other books in....

The Cole Brothers series

Book 1: *Montana Christmas Magic*

Book 2: *Montana Rancher's Kiss*

Book 3: *The Montana Cowboy's Heart*

Available now at your favorite online retailer!

More books by Kaylie Newell

The Harlow Brothers series

The Harlow brothers learned at a young age that family is what you make of it. Born on the wrong side of the tracks and abandoned by their father, Judd, Luke and Tanner have grown into remarkably tough men who are jaded by life. But when they come together as guardians of their orphaned half-sister, they'll find that love is what you make of it, too. As they learn how to be the fathers they never had, their carefully constructed walls begin to crack. But it will take three strong women to tear those defenses down for good, and show them what true happiness looks like.

Book 1: *Tanner's Promise*

Book 2: *Luke's Gift*

Book 3: *Judd's Vow*

The Elliotts of Montana series

Book 1: *Christmas at Sleigh Bell Farm*

Book 2: *Betting on the Bull Rider*

Available now at your favorite online retailer!

About the Author

For Kaylie Newell, storytelling is in the blood. Growing up the daughter of two writers, she knew eventually she'd want to follow in their footsteps. She's now the proud author of over a dozen books, including the RITA® finalists, *Christmas at The Graff* and *Tanner's Promise*.

Kaylie lives in Southern Oregon with her husband, two daughters, a blind Doberman, and two indifferent cats.

Thank you for reading

The Montana Cowboy's Heart

If you enjoyed this book, you can find more from all our great authors at TulePublishing.com, or from your favorite online retailer.

TULE
PUBLISHING

Made in United States
North Haven, CT
30 December 2024